A TALE OF STRAWBERRIES

Also by Pamela Hill:

Flaming Janet
Shadow of Palaces
Marjorie of Scotland
Here Lies Margot
Maddalena
Forget Not Ariadne
Julia
The Devil of Aske
The Malvie Inheritance
The Incumbent
Whitton's Folly
Norah Stroyan
The Green Salamander
Tsar's Woman
Homage to a Rose
Stranger's Forest
Daneclere
Daughter of Midnight
Fire Opal
Knock at a Star
A Place of Ravens
This Rough Beginning
The House of Cray
The Fairest One of All
Duchess Cain
Bride of Ae
The Copper-Haired Marshal
Still Blooms the Rose
The Governess
Children of Lucifer
Sable for the Count
My Lady Glamis
Venables
The Sisters
Digby
Fenfallow
The Sutburys
Jeannie Urquhart
The Woman in the Cloak
Artemia
Trevithick
The Loves of Ginevra
Vollands
A Dark Star Passing
The Brocken
The Sword and the Flame
Mercer
The Silver Runaways
Angell & Sons
Aunt Lucy
O Madcap Duchess
The Parson's Children
The Man from the North
Journey Beyond Innocence
The Charmed Descent
The Inadvisable Marriages
Curtmantle
The Small Black Knife
Saints' Names for Confirmation
Murder in Store
The Supplanter
Countess Isabel
The Lion's Daughter
Bailie's Wake
The Gods Return
Alice the Palace
Venus Rising

As Sharon Fiske:
Summer Cypress
Widow's Veil

A Tale of Strawberries

Shakespeare's Journeys in Scotland

Pamela Hill

UNITED WRITERS
Cornwall

UNITED WRITERS PUBLICATIONS LTD
Ailsa, Castle Gate, Penzance, Cornwall.

British Library Cataloguing in Publication Data:
A catalogue record for this book is available from the British Library.

ISBN 1 85200 113 5

Printed in Great Britain by
United Writers Publications Ltd
Cornwall.

To Nanette, Billy,
Rosemary and David.

AUTHOR'S NOTE

It is assumed that Shakespeare went to Scotland, if only from the information in *Macbeth*. If so, it is probable that such a visit was made in the years 1592-3, when theatres in London were closed because of plague. Shakespeare would be in time to hear the rumours about the murder of a young earl in February of that year, would also meet the suspected murderer Huntly and his possible instigator, the enigmatic King James VI. That king's fears, jealousies and devious forms of revenge would give Shakespeare many stories, some of which have been used in his plays, including *Othello*. The people he would meet, some of whom remembered the king's dead mother Mary Stuart, and the fate of those who had helped or hindered her and her son, are varied enough to make a kind of tapestry.

All characters in this story are real except the Spanish steward Gomez, who may well have existed among the survivors of the Armada washed up in the far north. I wanted to bring him in because of the history of Fair Isle knitting. The player of Grumio would also have his own name, which I do not know except that he was a member of

Pembroke's troupe. It is highly probable that someone got drunk on Edinburgh whisky. Shakespeare, as related, was back again in London by Christmas 1594.

The matter of cryptic messages in Shakespeare's plays has been brilliantly dealt with by Father Peter Milward, S.J., in his book on the subject, published by the St. Austin Press.

P.H.

THE STEWART KINGS
(simplified)

Robert II Stewart of Scots, grandson of Robert I Bruce
m. (1) Elizabeth Mure of Rowallan

John (Robert III)

Robert Duke of Albany

The Avandales —— Descent from Robert I Bruce by a younger daughter

James I Stewart
m. Joan Beaufort who m. (2) James Stewart the Black Knight of Lorn

James II

6 dau.

'Hearty James' Earl of Buchan

James III

The Stewarts of Traquair
(bastard line) →

James IV
m. 1503 Margaret, dau. to Henry VII. She m. (2) Archibald Douglas,
6th Earl of Angus and
(3) Henry Stewart of
Avandale, later
Lord Methven → ?

James V m. (2) Marie de Guise

Margaret Douglas m. Matthew Stewart,
Earl of Lennox

by Margaret
Erskine –
James, later
Earl and
Regent Moray,
m. Agnes
Keith, k. 1570

Mary Queen of Scots m. (2) Henry Lord Darnley

Charles

Elizabeth, m. The Bonnie
Earl of Moray,
James Stewart of Doune,
k. 1591-2

James VI and I m.
Anna of Denmark 1589

Lady Arbella Stuart
d. 1615

The later Stuarts, the
Hanoverians and the
present royal family.

THE RUTHVEN CLAIM

(simplified – [Pronounced 'Riven'])

Archibald Douglas, 6th Earl of Angus m. (1) Margaret Hepburn d. 1513
(2) Janet Stewart of Traquair
by handfasting, 1513

Janet m. Patrick
Lord Ruthven

William Ruthven 1st Earl
of Gowrie, executed 1584
m. Dorothea Stewart

Many children including
the two sons killed in the
Gowrie Conspiracy of
1600. Persecution of the
family continued till 1624.

m. (3) 1514 Queen Margaret Tudor,
widow of James IV.
One daughter born 1515.
Divorce 1528, by which time the
Queen had married, thirdly, Henry
Stewart of Avandale, later Lord Methven.
He had, possibly by the Queen (d. 1541)

by Janet Stewart
of Atholl (later his
wife) several children

all of whom were
legitimated in 1551.

Dorothea
m. Gowrie

Margaret
m. Lennox

Henry Lord
Darnley m.
Queen Mary

James VI & I
d. 1625

THE BOTHWELL MARRIAGES

Patrick, 3rd Earl, m. Agnes Sinclair

James, 4th Earl, Duke of Orkney,
d. 1578 at Dragsholm in Denmark.
He m. 1565-6 Lady Jean Gordon
Huntly. She divorced Bothwell to
let him marry Queen Mary, 1567,
and m. (2) in 1573, Alexander, Earl
of Sutherland, who died in 1594.
She married (3) in 1599, Alexander
Ogilvy of Boyne, d. in a few years.
Lady Jean lived to be 84, dying in
1629 at Dunrobin. She left children
by her second marriage.

Janet m. John Stewart, natural
son of James V. She made
later marriages.

Francis
(the Wizard Earl)

descent

CONTENTS

Part One

THE BONNIE EARL

ON a chilly Fife evening in early February of 1592, a young man of twenty-six, so handsome that heads turned to look at him if he rode by, was seated with his long legs – he was tall – stretched out before one of the new closed stoves he had caused to be installed with other improvements now he had decided to risk taking up residence here in Donibristle, within reach of the court. Stoves of the kind were among the luxuries obtainable now in Scotland with the long peace and the king's Danish marriage.

The young earl of Moray was enjoying the heat, having had a long cold ride earlier and before that, having spent much time in the open for good reasons. He had dined downstairs tonight with his sheriff and the rest, however, then had said he had private business. In fact he wanted to be alone for a while. He had hardly had time to grieve for his young wife's death, already eight months ago; the baby, called Francis, would be almost weaned. He had not heard the news at once.

He must rid himself of the certainty he had that danger still threatened. It was some time now since the king had ordered Huntly to bring him in for questioning. If they had been determined to take him, it could have been done long ago. He had been openly in the company of Francis Bothwell, and openly down at Traquair. The latter place should have been safe enough, except for what he'd heard there. As a result, he'd left and had ridden again north.

Outside it had been harsh, even for the time of year. Galloping hard against the bitter wind that had chosen to blow today across the grey, tossing Firth from beyond Edinburgh, even a south-easter had felt icy. He had avoided the capital with its warm inns, as too near the court again quite yet. Instead of crossing by the ferry he had come by way of Stirling, from where he had been skulking – no other word for it – with his Stewart kin. It was a long way round from Traquair.

Down there in the Border country it had been mild, making it possible to walk about on the grass outside the fair turreted house with William Stewart, laird now the last had died. Traquair was remote enough to have allowed certain things to happen in the past that might, now he knew of them, form a part of the danger. Maybe not; William Stewart had dared to shelter, besides himself, one other persecuted inmate; the unfortunate Lady Gowrie, still driven from pillar to post. The king no doubt had his reasons hidden in his mysterious and retentive mind. For Dorothea Stewart to have married a Ruthven, whoever her mother was, remained an offence even now, with her husband the earl dead these eight years on the block. His widow was not permitted to make use of the town house in Perth, though her two eldest sons might do so. Some of the other children she had borne Gowrie were kept about court. Two of the daughters were in attendance on the new queen.

He hadn't set eyes on Dorothea Gowrie on this visit, and could truthfully say so if asked. She had remained upstairs, herself afraid the king might hear of it if they met; it was known Moray was a fugitive. By now, at her age, she was in constant fear of shadows, though this one might be solid enough. He might come to such a state himself, was near it now. The whole thing could, after all, be no more than a black dog on his shoulder.

There were certainties, however. Walking on the shaved Traquair grass with William Stewart it had been possible to see, in the clear day, a difference in him; deepened lines of grief for the friend he had truly loved, Gowrie, by whose side he had walked to the block and, later, seen the headless body buried. It had happened so swiftly there had been no leisure for feeling at the time. Feeling had come with belief, nurtured and soured over the years. Words spilled out of the laird of Traquair as they walked together on the open stretch of grass before the house, one place clear of eavesdroppers.

"What had the king in his mind agin Gowrie? It could never ha'e been a plot to seize Stirling Castle for his wife's sake, as was spread. That canna be ta'en even with armies, and Gowrie had nane. Nor is it that James himsel' canna forgi'e his ain seizure nine years back, when the Ruthvens and Mar held him prisoner a year in the tower he will no longer name. That was to rid the country o' Esmé Stuart, when he cam' frae France to plan, he and Arran, to bring back Queen Mary to reign alongside her son." There had been a portrait made then of the mother and son together, they not having met since the king was in his cradle. James had been painted wearing the oriflamme of France.

"The king loved Esmé overmuch, they say." Huntly, now, was married to the dead French meddler's daughter, having helped the king meantime to escape from durance. The king had never forgotten it, although by that time they'd forced him to sign a decree for Esmé's exile. James VI had heaped Huntly with favours later and since. He had given Gowrie, a Ruthven, an earldom, then executed him. Nobody could be certain of anything. Even Huntly had been warded in prison three times, for the look of the thing as he was a papist. He himself, of a family strong for reform, might be imprisoned likewise; if that was all, he would miss the comforts of this stove. He placed his foot against it, savouring the warmth. He thought again of William Stewart, looking with prudence over his shoulder even on the open grass, talking of causes begun eight years since, maybe long before that.

"The reason for't is such as canna now be mended. Not all ken the Ruthvens o' Gowrie ha'e as guid a right, by double descent, to the croun o' England as James Stuart himsel'. That he hopes to be the auld queen's heir is weel kent. He let his ain mither's heid fa' beneath an English axe wi' never a word said till after, when they say he wrote in protest. Protest! The kings afore him would ha'e ridden south in armour, wi' cannon and swords."

"The last who did that got himself killed at Flodden. This sixth James will see to't that he dies in his ain bed, be it north or south."

Moray heard his own voice, grown dry and cautious like an older man's. He wished Traquair had not told him of the Gowrie claim. Evidently he felt the need to unburden himself fully; the rest came out of him as they walked. Dorothea, who had used to boast of it, was maybe the daughter of old Queen Margaret Tudor, James IV's widow, legally married to a third young man who happened to be Moray's kinsman.

The queen's earlier, second marriage, made soon after Flodden, was doubtful in law. Archibald Douglas, grandson of the old earl of Angus, one of the few to ride home from the fatal field, had paused at Traquair on hearing that his young Hepburn bride had died in childbirth. He had handfasted wild Janet Stewart, who bore him a daughter accordingly. Thereafter, on acquiring the title, Angus had ridden to Edinburgh to a court still in mourning, and had made a secret marriage with the widowed queen, fancying himself as ruler of Scotland for her young son James V. Although they fell out soon, the queen bore him a daughter also, who later became the mother of Darnley. If the Lady Margaret Douglas, countess of Lennox, was illegitimate, so was half James Stuart's claim to England through his father. A handfasting in Scotland meant a marriage, and wild Janet had betaken herself down to Greenwich to beard Henry VIII in person and tell him so. However that fearsome monarch had liked Angus, by then his guest, and had refused to disinherit his half-royal niece.

Knowledge of the matter was gunpowder such as had been intended to blow up the king's father at Kirk o' Field, except that Darnley's Douglas kin had already drawn his neck before the blast wakened Edinburgh. It was best to pretend to know nothing.

Meantime it was safest to leave Traquair. Moray had after all risked, in the end, coming home to his own house. Either the king would send to take him, or else not. The reason would be, for the time, less what he knew about the Ruthvens and Queen Margaret Tudor, the long-dead link who might gain James his English throne, but his own recent dealings with Francis Bothwell, his friend, a rebel born and maybe mad. Could a man not have liking for another, and call his son for him, without danger to his life? Even Bess's death up at Doune was not yet real. He blamed Huntly for preventing him from hearing of it in time.

Moray drained his wine-cup, half full still of what had been good hot spiced wine they'd brought, but it cooled quickly with the night's chill. However he was warmer now. How long he would be permitted to stay here in his own house in safety he could by no means tell; best make what he might of it while it could be done. A warm fire and a full belly were comforting, even though no matter what befell, Huntly was his foe and would see harm come to him if it might.

Huntly. He had always disliked the man, with his sly French-bred ways and his papistry. It went against anything he, with his reformed upbringing, had been taught to believe in. It was true his own kinsman, Ochiltree, had assured him lately that King James only wanted him for questioning, no doubt about Francis Bothwell's daft goings to and fro. To look straight in the royal eyes might be enough; those dark mournful heavy-lidded eyes, only likeness of the king's to his dead mother. It would be best to speak out boldly, whatever there was to say. There was bad blood with the Huntly clan since before his own birth, not only because his sept of the Avandale Stewarts was strong for reform. The Moray title itself had been taken away from the Huntlys in a great-grandfather's time, and they would not forget it. He himself held the title by right of his wife, the dead Regent's dead daughter.

That would be one grudge. Moreover he had been commissioned by the king – it was some years back – to hunt down Jesuits following the new Armada scare in England. That had been no more than a gesture to placate the old English queen. However Huntly had a brother, a Jesuit priest in France, who came over often, persuading souls to their undoing.

The king was lenient enough with Jesuits when caught; he had clapped Father Huntly in prison, not uncomfortably, more than once, and had done the same, for various reasons, to Huntly himself. Maybe there need be less anxiety on his own account than he now felt. The royal favour had been steady enough, and he should have contrived not to lose it; but how could he have refused that time to dance with the young queen?

The king had surprised everyone by venturing overseas to fetch his bride. It had been the worst storm in memory, and James had never taken ship before. He had found the Princess Anna of Denmark in a snowbound place in Norway, as her own journey had been delayed and so had the betrothal – the old queen of England had been angered by the publication, by Anna's father King Frederick, of the dying Bothwell's statement of Mary Stuart's innocence regarding the murder of Darnley. The marriage had been accomplished, the pair had returned briefly to Denmark to meet the royal court, there had been a second ceremony, and James VI brought his young queen home through an even wilder storm, so bad ships were sunk in Leith harbour. Nevertheless the royal couple were safe, and the queen crowned in state.

According to the evidence of a woman named Annis Simpson – Moray recalled it because by the king's especial mercy, she had been strangled afterwards before being burnt with the rest – a coven of Berwick witches had set out on the North Sea in sieves, raised the storm, but failed to drown the king because he was *un homme de Dieu*. Annis had said as much, and although she knew no French said more, in the king's ear; the very words he had whispered to his queen on their wedding night. The whole business was unchancy, and James deeply disturbed. Francis Bothwell, never averse to putting himself forward, had announced that he and no other was the witches' leader. He had been put in prison, but got out with flamboyant ease. He might be copying his uncle, who in Queen Mary's time had escaped the inescapable, namely by climbing down the steep rock-face of Edinburgh Castle. He must have had Francis' charm; small wonder the queen had been cozened to her undoing. Francis had the Stewart charm as well; his mother, by now the Mistress of Caithness and riding at the head of her own armies in the north, had been married first to Francis' father, a younger bastard of James V. That had been before the royal surname had begun to spell itself French fashion, with Queen Mary's education there and no letter 'w' in the language. His own, and that of all other descendants of Robert II, remained unchanged. He had Beaufort blood as well, from Queen Joan's second marriage, as little liked in Scotland as Queen Margaret Tudor's. As regarded high blood, he could hold up his head with Huntly or any noble among them all. It was one reason why his own marriage had been permitted, to the late Regent Moray's eldest daughter.

The young earl stared at a dark man's portrait, hanging on the whitewashed wall. The flicker of the stove gave the painted face a semblance of life, as if the stern lips moved above the narrow ruff of an earlier generation. Moray's father-in-law, from whom he took his title, had been known as the Good Regent by the victorious reformers. However as he rode in the street of Linlithgow twenty years back, a young man whose wife had been raped by his soldiery shot him. He had had a notable funeral, with the sermon preached by John Knox. There had been no sons of his grand Keith marriage, and Bess had inherited the title he himself now held in her right. The dead Regent, yet another James Stewart, had been the second known bastard of James V, who would have married his mother except that she was married already. Her son resembled what was known of her. The younger man stared at the erect dark head, the prudent long-nosed face, the air of probity which could, after all, be questioned; the elder Moray had betrayed his royal half-sister, who trusted him. He had greatly wanted to be king. In the end he had defeated her and caused her flight to England, to prison and, in the end, death.

Ruffs were less formal now. They were worn open at the throat, making it easier to breathe. However the room was growing stuffy. Moray loosed his doublet, then again surveyed his shapely legs in their French hose, noted for their skill in the dance. He was glad he had had them pull off his long, soft riding-boots on coming in with the sheriff. He had preferred to come here rather than to go to his brother Henry at nearby St. Colme, though the Donibristle house was newly plastered and needed drying out. For one thing it would have been known at once that he was at the castle. Here, for the time, he could be private.

He looked away from his father-in-law's portrait and thought of his wife. He had married Elizabeth Stewart eleven years ago, both of them being young. She could barely remember her father, and her mother by then was countess of Argyll. He had been given the choice of Bess or her younger sister, and had understandably chosen the heiress. He had also, even then, been given both girls' wardship. The Regent's widow had borne her new earl sons. The sixth Argyll was kin to Moray's mother, with the same cold Campbell mind. The wardship had maybe been conveyed to console her for the disgrace of her late brother the fifth Argyll, who had lost Langside for Queen Mary by fainting at the outset of the fray. But for that, Mary Stuart, a papist, might still be on her throne. Instead, her coffin lay at Peterborough, the body separated from the head.

Well, things had turned out as they had. He and Bess had been happy enough, witness five children in eleven years. Bess. He still hadn't had time to remember that she was dead. She would have liked to see her father's portrait on the wall of the new house. He had had it hung there to please her. She had told him how, as a child, she remembered seeing the bloodstained body carried in at last to Linlithgow while her mother, the Lady Agnes, had been upstairs trying on Queen Mary's heart-shaped coifs, one with drop pearl trimming, she'd left behind when she fled in a black wig after Langside. The Lady Agnes had kept her fingers on as much of the queen's gear as she might; there had been shoes he could remember, with small curled heels, in green leather, and M and FII embroidered on each in gold, initials of the queen and her first husband when they had briefly been king and queen of France.

The black French pearls had had to be sent south by request. He'd heard old Queen Bess had bought them after the execution, so they would have been worth keeping. The Lady Agnes's family, the Keith Earls Marischal, was so ancient nobody was certain when it had begun. Bess had conveyed that blood to his sons. If anything happened to himself, the title was safe.

The room was growing warmer still, the stove smoking more than somewhat. He still thought of Bess, and knew anger at having been prevented from being at the death-bed. Only his mother had been with her when young Francis was being born to them at Doune. No doubt James, the heir, had been led in to see Bess die. There was no such forbidding now of being with the dying after they had made a last confession; such things were no longer countenanced.

There was silence still, except for an occasional murmur of talk from below. How warm it had grown! If the stove didn't stop smoking, he would send for someone; but meantime there was a thing he wanted to look at. He let his hand stray to his opened doublet, inside which a folded object lay, and drew it out. It was worth looking at, but he seldom did so except when alone, as to be seen to do so might cause trouble. It was a gift from the young Danish queen. She had sent it by way of her waiting-woman, Mistress Twinelace, for having been so able a partner to her in the dance. The king himself, unable to dance, let alone walk unaided – his legs had been weak from birth – had been watching from the dais. He, Moray, and the tall fair-haired, long-nosed, white-skinned girl, who had surprisingly dark eyes, had danced high and disposedly, the tallest couple in the hall. He could still hear the sound of the fifes and rebecks. He had lifted Queen Anna by the waist and twirled her as was customary in a certain figure. She herself had a fine one for her age. The king had had her anointed at her coronation, to the fury of the Kirk. She had climbed back up beside James after the dance was over. It had been related afterwards what she had said, having learned Scots quickly. "He," – himself, Moray – "is the properest and most gallant man in the hall."

"Ye micht ha'e excepted me," had replied James Stuart drily.

That was another source of danger. It would be better if nobody knew of the gift. Moray's own tough old father, Lord Doune, dead only last year, had been one of Rizzio's murderers alongside old Ruthven, in the months before the king's birth. They had thrust, with the rest, at Queen Mary's body, seven months pregnant, with the intent to make her miscarry after they dragged the dying Italian secretary away. Darnley, her husband, had been privy to the plot. She'd saved her unborn child, and herself; Bothwell had been waiting in time with horses, and had carried her and the treacherous Darnley to safety, and later the prince had been born in Edinburgh Castle. He hadn't grown up like other children; his walk was unsteady and his tongue too big, so that he had to keep his lips clamped over it. They had blamed a drunken wet-nurse, but everyone knew it was the result of what his mother had endured before his birth. James VI would know it himself; he was no fool. Watching the dance, seeing the queen flushed and happy. *Your sire spoiled me in the womb, and now ye partner my bride while I sit alane*. His mind would work in such a fashion, deep and resentful.

He was a scholar and a poet. Moray could not have

matched him in any such way; his own feats were physical. The king had written verses to Danish Anna for long enough before they met, although some had maybe been intended for a young Murray girl they'd got for him during the year in the tower. That had been to try to turn his mind from the likes of Esmé Stuart, but when Esmé died the king mourned greatly, and brought his children from France, Huntly's bride among them.

Huntly. He must forget him by staring down at the unfolded gift. It was a handkerchief embroidered with strawberries, large and to be held in the hand Spanish fashion, as had been done a generation ago in England, in Bloody Mary's time. This, though, had been embroidered nearer home.

It was old. The heavy, creamy silk which made the ground had yellowed unevenly, as though it had maybe been stuffed for long at the back of some cupboard, forgotten with the years. The small fruit had been sewn in scarlet silk which with time had faded gracefully into different shades of vermeil, murrey-colour and russet and rose. The tiny yellow seeds showed evenly, and the green leaves and tendrils curled. Only an expert embroideress could have completed it. Queen Mary's mother had brought new strawberry plants with her from France when she came across to marry James V. They had flourished well in the soil of Fife. They had a pineapple flavour, different from the small wild strawberries he remembered plucking on the waysides as a child.

Strawberries. They would remind Mary Stuart of her mother, whom she had loved and whose long coffin she had received at last in Normandy before embarking, a widow of eighteen, to rule Scotland alone.

She had been a noted embroideress. Was this her work? If so, and it had escaped the Lady Agnes' foragings, how could the young Danish queen have received it, except from the king? If James had given it her, it had been impulsive and foolish of Anna to send it to himself, the properest man in the hall. She would not, of course, know the value James might set on the few things he had left of his mother's. His early tutors had brought him up to believe Mary a whore. Esmé Stuart would teach him otherwise about her. Esmé had been considered a danger, and this gift was a danger. He ought to destroy it, thrust it in the stove: but if James should ask him for its return, what then? In any case it was too fair a thing to destroy.

Moray folded it up again carefully, and replaced it in his doublet. It was so hot in the room now he felt uncomfortable, and the smoke was becoming thick. Maybe the builder had left loose stones or plaster, blocking the draught in the chimney. His throat was choking with it, despite the late wine. It was maybe folly not to have gone to St. Colme till all was ready.

He got up and strode to the door to open it. Beyond, the smoke was blanket-thick. There was a disturbance below. He called for the servants. Turning his head to the window, he saw a sudden creeping of flame below, brightening the darkness and blotting out the sea. He slung on his sword. They'd been incautious, drinking and chattering below, not keeping watch; and yet, this fire must have been laid ready, dry brushwood stacked about the walls. They would hope, his enemies, that by now he was abed, to burn in it. He hastened down, cursing because he was unshod.

"My lord! My lord! The house is afire! Come away, ye are betrayed! They are surrounding us!"

It was Dunbar the sheriff, halfway up the stairs. Moray had drawn his sword, and hastened towards the flames already licking at the outer door. Beyond it were dark figures, their blades lit by the creeping, growing wall of fire.

He must fight through it towards them; there was no way back. The sheriff followed, they leaped through the flames, then he saw the man's mouth open blackly in a scream as he fell wounded among their daggers. Behind, they were trying to put out the fire; Moray could smell the doused smoke, hear the hiss of water. He fought his way out through the searing heat that burned his soles, black by now from head to foot like an African; at least it hid one man's face from the rest, though his tall height would be known. His clothes were alight and he began, having gained the darkness, to run and at the same time to try and extinguish them by slapping at them with one hand, the other retaining his sword. Once he could reach St. Colme there would be protection. Maybe from there they had already seen the fire, and would come with aid.

He could hear the sea now faintly, smell it in nostrils distended like a stag's with fear. There was still the stench of scorched cloth about him. He knew what it was; his cap was on fire. He pulled at it with his hand, keeping his sword free in the other. A sword hampered running, but with good fortune he'd shaken them off.

He had not. They were waiting, more of them, at the turning which should have led to St. Colme. There was no escape now but by water, but he could swim. He ran in at last, feeling his clothes hiss and the icy Forth engulf him to the knees. The scorched tassel of his cap was caught once again by the shore wind, renewing a little spark. He should have thought of taking it off; they'd seen it in the darkness, and came grimly on. Between the light of the spark and the stars, the last thing James Moray saw was Huntly's weasel face. There was one other there, one of the many Gordons, or maybe an Ogilvie. There were nine Gordon brothers, and it didn't matter which. They slashed at his sword-arm, slowed as he was by the weight of the water. They slashed at his handsome face, slicing the nose, laying open one cheek. Moray felt the blood run down warmly, not yet aware of pain. The last thought that remained with him was that he would never be worth looking at again. Gasping, dying, his sword useless, he spat out words at Huntly from behind a curtain of blood.

"Ye ha'e spoilt a better face than your ain."

They hacked, stabbed, slew at last; then dragged the still bleeding body out of the water. "Lay him ayont the tide-line," said the Cock o' the North.

It was too cold to linger. Patrick Gordon, who feared fewer things than his brother, laid the two dead men, lord and sheriff, side by side, rifled both bodies methodically, then made off. Already there was a stirring, and lanterns lit, across at St. Colme, having seen the fire creep and grow about the doomed house at Donibristle. There was no need to wait to be recognised. The dark closed in as the Gordons rode off, while the high flames died to unwilling smoke round a place by now unfit for habitation.

The news that the Bonnie Earl was slain reached Edinburgh, then Doune. In the latter place, Moray's widowed mother sent for her grandchildren, told them curtly their father was dead and left them with the nurses, their faces bewildered; it was not long since they had lost their mother. She then rode south through the February weather, and on arrival demanded to see the face of her dead son.

By then the bodies had been taken to St. Giles's Kirk, and lay within the tomb of the Good Regent, awaiting burial. The churchwarden reluctantly lifted away the outer lid.

"We didna bury him, my leddy, till ye suld come."

He himself was trying not to feel sick. The warmth of the lamps – there were no popish candles now – had caused flies to awaken at this season from their sleep. They had made their way between the joints of lid and side, and had laid their eggs in the dead earl's wounds beside those already hatched after eight days' exposure on the Fife shore; no man had dared touch the bodies until the king sent word. By now the flesh was green, with heaving maggots. The slashed cheek had shrunk to reveal the bared gum and exposed teeth. Margaret Stewart, born Margaret Campbell, gazed down on the ruined face of what had been her eldest son, renowned for his manly beauty and tall height, his skill at the ring and the courtly dance. Being of the clan into which she had been born rather than the one she had married, her grief was cold, clear and far-sighted. "Leave him be for now," she said. "I will have a limner take his likeness as it is, and send it to the king."

She turned and went out, making no further sign; such things were done with, and she was of the reformed faith. The churchwarden made himself stare at the displaced brass memorial to the Good Regent, engraved in excellent Latin put together, at the time of the Linlithgow murder, by Master George Buchanan, sometime tutor to the king. Everyone knew James was involved in this death, and there was much anger in the town. The Bonnie Earl had been a fine sight, riding down to Holyrood in his time, with his bugles winding and his spurs gleaming, and his bonnie face for all to see. The king was protesting sorrow, as he'd done about his own mother once it was too late, and saying Huntly had exceeded his orders, he'd only been told to bring the earl for questioning.

Nobody believed it. The earl and the young queen had made well-matched partners in the dance, while the king had sat glowering.

The king would be jealous, treacherous like his father Darnley. Some said Rizzio was his father. Others said Rizzio had been Darnley's lover. There would always be gossip.

And the Good Regent? The churchwarden, who like all godly folk read his Bible, recalled a text which had struck him at the time of the Linlithgow murder. *Bastard slips take no deep root*.

When he could be undisturbed, Huntly took out an object retrieved from the dead earl's clothing, most of which had been unfit to preserve. This handkerchief, however, had taken little harm except for sea-water stains, and maybe some blood. It was a fine and costly thing, such as in the ordinary way he would have given to his young wife, Henrietta. However the blood made it unsuitable to be held in her white hand, dangling against her skirts in the Spanish fashion come up briefly out of England after King Philip had left the late Queen Mary Tudor to die alone. Fashions were slow to reach the north parts, although Henrietta's mother continued to bring the latest of them from France.

No, the handkerchief was unsafe to keep. It would be the late queen's work and the king had given it to Danish Anna after her coronation, very grand she'd been, in purple velvet. It had been foolish of her to part with it to the handsome earl. The less said about it now the better; yet, it was too good a thing to be destroyed.

Huntly knew where he would send it, and to whom. He put it away carefully meantime, not attempting to wash out the stains. Some harm might come to it, the colours might run, or it might rot. His sister Jean would take care of it. It was maybe fitting that she should, having let her erstwhile husband Bothwell marry the late Queen Mary here. Jean had waited many years before marrying again. Now she was in Sutherland, and there the precious thing should go by way of his brother James the priest, next time he visited Scotland. It was true harm might befall it if James was taken and put in prison again, being searched for mass-gear, but he was a wise man and would know what best to do.

Priests had a great lack; they couldn't lie with their wives. He himself liked greatly to bed Henrietta. He would do so again tonight. It was said the king thought of her as a daughter. Their wedding had been by far grander than the king's own, and at Holyrood itself, when the bride was thirteen. He himself had voyaged to bring her over, and see his kin in France. The king had liked to hear of it; he had loved Henrietta's father, elegant Esmé Stuart, Sieur d'Aubigny, duke of Lennox. That was what the king's favour could mean. He, Huntly, could be assured of the royal protection in the late matter of Moray. The ignorant commons had made a ballad of it. How did it go?

O, wae betide ye, Huntly,
And wherefor did ye sae?
I bade ye treat him gently,
And forbade ye him to slay.

He was a braw gallant,
And he rade at the glove;
And the bonnie earl o' Moray,
He was the Queen's luve.

O, lang may his ladye sit
High in the Castle Doune,
Ere she see the earl o' Moray
Come soundin' through the toun.

The legend would endure, wrongly, of course. In any case he had nothing to fear. He and the king understood one another. There were a great many other verses, and always the chorus about the earl's lady, who was dead like her earl, the late godly commissioner to hunt down Jesuits.

Part Two

THE WAYFARER, 1592-3

HE had been told Northumbria was mystic and misty, with the last coming down suddenly and without warning. However a gale had blown up instead, with bursts of rain. He held his short frieze cloak about him, wishing he'd brought a cap; his domed head was balding and the rain fell on it and ran down past the remaining length of hair inside his collar. His slightly prominent, perceptive hazel eyes, above the questing nose and passionate underlip, stared at the way ahead as far as one could see. The storm was, after all, one more interesting experience. He could use it in a play, later. Meantime, it was unlikely anyone would be out in it unless by accident. At that rate he might not find what he had come out to search for, leaving the troupe and property-cart at the inn. He sniffed the wet fresh air thankfully, free of the smells of sweat and old wigs and grease-paint. It had been best to bring nobody with him, say nothing of where he was bound. In plain fact he was uncertain of where that might be, or if it might be at all. Here in the north parts the old faith was still practised, but any priests left after the old king's hangings lived in hiding, their whereabouts known only to those who could be trusted, who could give the sign he, William Shakespeare, knew.

He was not, at any rate, hungry. There had been a good inn at which to rest with Pembroke's men last night after leaving Peterborough, or was that the day before? Time went slowly on a slow journey, taking turns with the horses or else swaying with the rest in the cart. By now, among the green uninhabited country, it was possible to forget London and the way the theatres were closed a second summer running because of the plague. In the deserted streets nobody would venture out; folk stayed shut in their houses, hearing the creaking of wheels that collected the dead. *Bring out your dead*. That was London, flower of cities all, at present. His patron the earl had understandably not wanted to pay an idle troupe, but didn't want to disband them. Pembroke had given him money for the journey, but he hoped to repay it after playing to great houses in Scotland. Their new queen was said to enjoy entertainment, and their king was a poet and had a poets' circle. He, Will, not venturing plays when there was nowhere to put them on, had written two long epics only in the last two years. Both were bitter against women, Venus and Lucrece. He himself was suffering from unrequited love. It suited his mood well enough to battle with the driving wind and rain.

The Scots themselves had lost a battle somewhere here among the green rising round hills.

There had been a storm then, and darkness at noon. It had been a place called Flodden. The old king's first queen had been left in command while he went off to fight in golden armour in France, thinking himself Harry Fifth over again. There had been great rejoicing at the Scots' defeat, and their king had been killed, the one who'd married his own old queen's aunt, Margaret Tudor. Queen Catharine had been proud of herself as a general, but they said the king was jealous, because her victory had been greater than his, and that that had been the beginning of discord between them.

He'd paused in Peterborough himself to visit Queen Catharine's tomb there, and nearby the one of Mary, Queen of Scots. She must have been a tall woman. Her story would make a play he dared not write.

Shakespeare thought, as he walked on against the gale, of Mary's son James VI, whom he hoped to meet; he had letters of introduction from Pembroke, also one to the earl of Huntly. The Pembroke family were related to Huntly in a strange way; the king who had lost Flodden had earlier invaded England on behalf of a fair-haired young man who said he was one of the missing sons of Edward IV. So convincing had the young man's tale been that the king, James IV, had given him a bride of royal descent, for two of the second earl of Huntly's wives were descended from Robert II, the Bruce's grandson, and one of them had been a princess as well. The bride had been very beautiful, and when the pretender, whom they said was really a Fleming named Warbeck, was hanged by old Henry VII, it was said he asked no other comfort than the Scots bride's company. Her name had been Lady Katherine Gordon, and after Henry VII died she married again, and yet again to a Welsh knight whose daughter by his first marriage had a son who became the new earl of Pembroke by yet another creation. It was unimportant except that, at this moment, he himself had a letter which might well gain him entry, even a bed, at Huntly House in the Canongate of Edinburgh.

The thought of a warm dry bed was welcome, even now. It still blew and roared. *Howl, winds, and crack your cheeks*. Such lines would come to him now and again, to be stowed away for future use. His mind teemed with ideas, but it was needful to please his patrons for the time. He had a family to support; his bankrupt father John, ruined with recusancy fines although he had earlier been a prosperous glove-maker and burgess, at one time high bailiff, of Stratford. There was

Susanna his joy, born six months after his marriage so that of course everyone had talked, but she was learning to run to him; and the twins, Hamnet and Judith, suckling now at Anne's sturdy breasts. He was glad Anne wasn't a fine lady and could feed her own children. He wanted greatly to see his son again, called after a prosperous citizen in order, perhaps, to give the boy a future if things turned out ill for himself. He hoped they would not; he was twenty-eight years old, had health and sight, could entertain high and low with his wit and use it to make ever more money and send some home. He'd sickened of a schoolmaster's life and had risked coming to London. He'd begun by holding horses' heads, then had progressed to paying boys for holding them. "I'm Shakespeare's boy, sir," was enough to ensure that the horse would still be there, safe and sound, when my lord came back for it. He had met lords and commons. He had seen the old queen, rouged and bewigged, pass by, with a long red jewel pinned in the wig and her face twenty years older since the death of Mary Stuart. It showed in spite of the paint. When Gloriana died, this odd king to whom he was going might well be ruler of a united country. The only other likelihood was an unknown young woman in the Midlands.

The rain had eased a little. He was uncertain where he was; one low treeless hill was the same as the next. If he saw a dwelling, he'd ask the way; but there was nothing here, and nobody. The Conqueror had said he'd make Northumbria a desert, and had done it, but the grass grew over. Later the Scots had come, lastly the king who'd lost Flodden. Before that he'd burned and raided; a ruined chapel or two still showed, like stone skeletons. Lady Katherine Gordon had ridden with her husband south, and must have seen the burnings. He might ask Huntly concerning it, or else not; it depended on what the man was like.

Old Pembroke had made one of his pithy comments and had said that Will, in Scotland, might keep his ears open concerning the recent murder of a handsome young earl to whom the new queen was said to have given a handkerchief embroidered with strawberries. Will had best keep that part, he said, to himself; he'd learned of it from Huntly. The image had stayed in Will's mind and would not leave it; again, lines had come to him he would use later.

Have you not seen a handkerchief
Spotted with strawberries, in your wife's hand?
Husband: *I gave it her; t'was my first gift.*

Something of the kind. The plot might involve a jealous husband, someone out of the common run; maybe with a difference that made him constantly aware of himself as different. There was small leisure to work on it at the moment, might not be any for long enough; but the fact of a notion raised him out of the valley of despondency. All he'd been able to think of was episodes of violence to women; ravishing, a tongue cut out, hands cut off to prevent naming the ravisher. An audience might love it or loathe it. In the meantime the light play he had more or less ready, called for now *The Taming of a Shrew*, might serve to entertain the court. A boy would act the Shrew, and be beaten.

Had James Stuart beaten his queen for giving away the handkerchief? It was unlikely; from all one heard, the man was less violent than subtle. His poetry was said to be better than that of either of his parents, and both had been notable; Lord Darnley, at the age of nine, had given a Latin treatise he'd written to Queen Mary Tudor, his mother's friend. James VI's poetry had gushed up like a fountain after what must have been a brutal upbringing. His tutor had been a grim Calvinist, who doubtless whipped him; he had never been allowed to know his mother, as his father had been murdered and the Scots queen married the murderer. The whole tale had eclipsed their own queen's earlier scandal, when Leicester's wife was found dead at the foot of a staircase.

There was no shortage of material for plays, but one had to be careful. If the young queen, beaten or not, fancied his productions, it would have been worth bringing his troupe north through this green morass. Will could hear his boots squelch in it. He was soaked through; it was time to go back to the inn, if he could find the way.

The queen of Scots' last husband, Bothwell, had died mad, they said in appalling conditions in Denmark. As for Queen Mary herself, Gloriana had kept her in prison eighteen years. There had been plot after plot to rescue her, some intended to kill the queen of England and place Mary on the throne. That had caused her death in the end. His own mother had been hauled before the magistrate, Sir Thomas Lucy, and questioned concerning one of the plots, not the last. Her maiden name was Arden, and she was kin to the Somervilles. He himself had been whipped by order of the same magistrate, as a lad, for poaching deer. In earlier times he would have lost a hand or an eye; but he had used his hand, and his eye, to write a squib on the word lousy.

Hope appeared among the uncharted green places; a figure flapping with wet, like himself. The man was very old, his white beard blowing. He was making his way with a staff and talking to himself. A madman, an old madman on a wild moor, in a storm. He might, however, point the way back to the inn.

"Friend, where am I?" Will called out against the wind.

The other paused in whatever tracks were leading him. Will held out his hand; then a thought came. The bald head, the ragged gear, resembled an early saint such as they had once had here; St. Cuthbert was well known, was said to have won Flodden. He saw the ancient's mouth drop open in a grin, revealing brown sparse teeth in the lower jaw.

"Lonnen's clarty." The thin voice was like a reed. Knowing nothing of the local way of speech Shakespeare guessed the topic to be the weather. His quick ear tried to adjust itself; there had to be a common root. He felt half his mind fly back to the properties; he hoped they'd had the sense to cover them with tarred cloth against the rain.

"I am lost," he said simply. "My inn is at Etal."

"I ken Etal. Durham's better, though the blessed body divvint be there naa."

Durham had been despoiled three years before the Pilgrimage of Grace, after which hundreds had hung on gibbets up here for opposing the king's reformation. Will raised a hand against the wind and made the sign of the Trinity. The other replied with the sign of the cross.

"I kenned as sune's I saw yee come yee wor one on us," he said, smiling. "Divvint tell aal men."

"Never that. It's the same in the south." Since the pope had excommunicated Elizabeth Tudor it had been hard to be a Catholic and be thought loyal. Nonetheless the Armada had been defeated under the command of Lord Howard of Effingham, a papist. Will thought of the Little Ease in the Tower, in which a man could neither sit, stand nor lie; they'd kept the martyred Jesuit, Edmund Campion, in it four days and nights before doing worse things to him. He had kept a high courage, even cheerfulness, through torture and the final gruesome death meted out to priests in England. James VI in Scotland was more lenient, at least so far. Strong clans like that of Huntly were still papist. No doubt

James had to balance their support against the Knoxian reformers who had ruined his childhood, at the same time taking care not to offend the English queen who had, in earlier times, financed them against her rival Mary Stuart.

As they walked, Will made his confession to the priest, Father Colum. It mattered little whether his relations of his sins, the hunger for the dark lady, his hesitancy about supporting the old faith openly for fear of losing support in high places, were understood; he was repentant, and received absolution. It would not be possible to attend Mass, which would be held in a certain place on the Sunday following; by then, he hoped to be in Edinburgh, and was told, in the difficult dialect, to go to Father James, who was there from overseas at present. It took some time to elicit the fact that he was the earl of Huntly's brother, and would be most easily met in evenings at a certain tavern in the Grassmarket, with his hat pulled over his eyes.

Bewildered, and pleased, by as much coincidence, Will pressed silver into the old priest's hand. The other gestured to him to kneel, which he did on the soggy ground. Father Colum then brought out what lay beneath his ragged robe under his beard; a pyx, and from it he took the Body of Christ and laid it in Will's mouth. It was the first time he had been able to receive communion since his boyhood. He was much moved.

"Gude ga wi' yee," said the old man, and went on his own way now the thatch of Etal showed through the persisting rain. Will hastened back and had the inn-wife strip him and wring out his clothes to dry before the fire, wrapping him meantime in a plaid woven from sheep's wool the reivers had brought from Scotland. The mutton they ate that night was no doubt from there as well. There was still coming and going across the Border over such things, despite the Wardens of the Marches.

He had delayed their journey by a day, but the rain would have slowed it. He did not regret the encounter with the old man on the moor. That image also would remain with him, at the back of his mind, to be used at some date, but not yet. Also, he had grown used to Father Colum's way of speaking, enough to understand what he had meant by the blessed body no longer in Durham. He had thought at first the old man meant the Sacrament, but he had been referring to the body of St. Cuthbert, miraculously preserved over the centuries, which when he had been a young ordinand he had seen wrenched roughly from its shrine by King Henry's commissioners who broke one of the legs. "They was afeard then, and left it on a table. When they came for't it wasna there." The brown teeth had grinned again. "Three allus knaws where 'tis, and the bones they put back in the shrine are other. Three allus knaws. I saw his face, with shrawd on't the holy wumman Verca wove. It wouldna come away, but I saw his cleavit chin and his turned-up nose through't. Five layers of silk they had him in, some from Holy Land where they took him after dragon ships came to Lindisfarne. Dragons flying through the mist, folk thought they saw. That was the first on 'em, and they got much gold, but him they divvn't get, nor ever will." He added that he was eighty-three years old, and could remember.

Shakespeare found himself lying in the inn-bed that night, between three snoring fellows, and thinking of the meticulous mind of Henry VIII. That king had not ordered the destruction of St. Cuthbert's body, because Cuthbert had obeyed a king by unwillingly becoming a bishop. On the other hand, at Canterbury a saint who had disobeyed a king had been sentenced to have his bones ground to powder and thrown into the Stour, and King Henry had ridden down twice in person to see that it had been done. All the same, they whispered that it had not; that, again, it had been done with other bones, and that St. Thomas Becket lay somewhere undisturbed. Shakespeare remembered a thing his father John had said, at the time still stitching, with his craftsman's fingers, at well-tanned calf's leather for a lady's glove, with gems and silver thread on the gauntlet. "St. Thomas made a joke to his Welsh clerk about how his behind stuck out, jutting beneath his alb when he fastened on his girdle. If they find jutting pelvic bones, they're his."

There had been a legend, later denied, that Becket's mother had been Syrian. Hottentots had lived in Syria in early centuries, with the jutting behinds. It was the kind of idea that came to him now, in the middle of the night, and would be of no use to anybody. It was better to remember the strawberry handkerchief given away to a handsome earl by a foolish queen, and the earl's murder. He would learn more about that in the taverns of Edinburgh. Tomorrow, if it was dry, the property-cart should make better speed.

The rain stopped, and they continued their journey, though a mist sprang up and slowed it; later they came to a place of high rocks and a waterfall. Will was still reflecting on the encounter with the old priest on the moor. It would lead to others by way of Father James, unless he had left the country. His goings back and forth must involve many disguises.

He beheld Edinburgh at last, a bowl of yellow filth seen from this height, smoke belching from many chimneys. Nevertheless the air still blew clean and cool from the sea, and maybe there was no plague as far north. If the city was in danger, he would travel on to some of the great houses and castles further up into unknown country, the country of the clans. The inn-folk he had left behind on the Border had called themselves Armstrongs, neither Scots nor English, owing loyalty only to themselves. They claimed to be descended from a fairy and a bear. There would be other stories the further north one went. He was beginning to take note of everything he saw; the descending path, the blue Forth in the distance, the hills beyond. There were no such hills in England. The speech here, as they passed bothies, was different again from that of Northumbria; broader, almost a foreign language. He must accustom his ear.

They descended into the narrow, jumbled wynds, and he asked the way to the Canongate. He parted with the rest, leaving the cart in charge of a trusted man, and followed the street up beyond a towered palace with green grass about it, and a chapel. Holyrood; there had been a king's vision here, of a crucifix between a stag's horns. He had built an abbey on the place. His Border abbeys – they had passed two on the way – lay in ruins since King Henry's raids fifty years ago. Here, though, the abbey was still a thing of splendour, with the palace standing foursquare alongside. James IV had built it, he'd been told, to be nearer the folk than up at the castle.

It was growing dark by now. Lit torches, bright and steady in their sconces against the grey walls, their yellow flares flung this way and that by the wind, showed him Huntly House. Two Highlanders in saffron shirts stood guard, the first he'd seen. Will approached, and asked for the earl, showing Pembroke's letter. The guards stared, and one said something in Gaelic. Neither could read, but the seal looked important. They nodded him in past the door.

Huntly was alone, drinking at a table. He wore a velvet coat and his head was bare. Shakespeare disliked the look of him, but his speech was hospitable enough once he had scanned Pembroke's letter. "Ye ha'e come far," the earl said, and asked if he had dined; and having learned that he had not, ordered bread and meat to be brought, and a stoup of wine. Will drank the wine thankfully; it was good, from France. He answered questions about the health of the Pembrokes, father and son.

"That was a late creation," said the earl of Huntly comfortably, knowing his own was older. "It was made, I believe, on a battlefield. It is doubtful which of us has the more battles to relate, ourselves or the English. Have ye fought, Master Shakespeare? Are ye apt with a spear?"

"My wars have been of words only. I hope to entertain yourself, and maybe the king and queen."

"The queen is at Dunfermline. There has been some little trouble between her and the king. He himself is at Holyrood, and the morn ye sall meet." The slight altering of terms and vowels intrigued Shakespeare; the morn, sall, the pronunciation of doubtful as dootfa'. He would get used to it. He hoped the players would make themselves understood. It might perhaps be needful to resort to mime, like the old Greeks. There were masks in the cart. As usual, he was concerned with its safety; but there was little enough worth stealing, the stuff was old. In any case he could improvise. There was *The Shrew*, but also *The Two Gentlemen of Verona* and *All's Well that Ends Well*. If there had been trouble between the king and queen, he had best avoid mention of marital strife.

Huntly droned on for a time; he was slightly drunk. He spoke of the last regent's head, stuck on the Tolbooth, crows having pecked it down to the eyeless skull. Morton, a Douglas, had helped murder the king's father long before, and the king's justice caught up with him in Esmé's day. Before that, when the king was still a child, his grandfather Lennox, an earlier regent, had been shot in the street like the Regent Moray. It was evidently less safe to be regent than king, but the king feared daggers, and wore padded clothing. "Ye will ken him by his hat."

He had seemed anxious to talk of murders and violence, but not of the death of the handsome young earl. Shakespeare held his peace. He would learn more about that in the taverns. It was known Huntly had carried out the murder; he'd heard as much in England. It was strange to be in the company of a murderer, and to be treated as an equal by an unknown lord. However he was at home in any company.

He slept between two others again, in a bed in the great house. He hadn't mentioned Father James to his own brother. It was possible the Jesuit was in the house, but the two brothers would go their different ways.

Next day Will set out early, before meeting the king. He wanted to ensure that the two young boys who would play Katherina and Bianca were comfortably lodged; he was responsible for them. He found them in a lodging in the Cowgate, not far off. The arrival of players from England had been noted by everyone, and they were not difficult to trace. However the good lady of the house had a fluent tongue and liked using it. He found it hard to get away, as talking to an Englishman was a thing that seldom happened to her, and her old mother, who was dead now, had told her of the wedding of the good King James IV to an English princess, and the streets here had run with wine, and the king had ridden past with his new queen on his saddle-bow, and her long red-gold hair hanging loose. That had been a golden time, and it was thought there would be no more war with England. "It cam'," said the woman, her dulled eyes looking at him as though she saw beyond. "It cam' in ten year. They were a' killed, the king and a' the lords, save the Douglas, and a pity it was he rade hame, for he mairrit the queen and did muckle harm after."

"Well, you have peace now," said Shakespeare, reflecting

that it was only peace of a kind. She nodded briskly, the laundered frill of her mutch shaking round her face. She had grey hair.

"Say what they may agin the king, we ha'e peace nou. He does as he will in his ain way, and it's never the way o' his fathers. I mind the deid queen, tall she was and bonnie, and her tall lord walking by, and Darnley's cap set jaunty on his gowden heid, as though he were king. They say that's what he was after, and the Douglases put him up to't, being his mither's folk, and a bad lot, after power for theirsel's. The queen's feyther put them to the horn, but back they cam' when he was deid. There's never been a king o' Scots lived to be auld. England they say is a fine country. I mind my man rade doun as far as York, but he didna reach London. I'm a widow these seeven year."

Will stemmed the flow and asked her to keep an eye on the two young lodgers, and said he must go to meet the king. At that the good woman's jaw fell open, and she wished him well with deep respect. The back of his head sensed her gaping after him as he made his way towards the palace, on whose grass a number of figures walked. Evidently the king was receiving. He brought out Huntly's letter, scrawled the night before. The earl might be present, or else might not. Will examined his fingernails to make sure they were clean. He had put on a fresh shirt, and had taken pains with his appearance, shaving closely.

He need not have troubled. He made out James VI at once, not only by his hat as the earl had said. The king's white hands, shapely like his mother's, were dirty. He wore a long robe, like an older man, and under it was maybe the padding Huntly had spoken of. The mournful Stuart eyes surveyed Will with some interest; there was nobody else much here today, except for two beautiful young men introduced as Lord Gowrie and his brother. The queen being absent, there were no women at court. Shakespeare heard himself being addressed in Latin, and replied with an answer he often gave.

"Sire, I know little Latin and less Greek."

"Then I am disappointed. I had thocht ye a scholar."

"Of the school of life." He must maintain the king's interest, or the journey would have been for nothing. The cautious royal face lost its unwillingness to be friends. This man was lonely.

They put on *All's Well* that evening at court, and the next was to be *The Two Gentlemen*. After the first play there was much applause, and Will found himself overcome with invitations to travel north and entertain great ladies in their castles. Among them was one from Huntly, who was present at the play. Master Shakespeare must have his troupe act before the young countess, and stay at their new house which was still being built in the French fashion. That was to be at Strathbogie, but there were other places first; and, meantime, the king beckoned with a soiled white finger.

"It would gi'e us pleasure were ye to come and see my verse, and those of the kings afore me." He sometimes remembered the royal 'we' and sometimes not; he was a mixture of appeal and, at any rate, some majesty. Will followed him to a closet, where he kept his books and privy papers in a tall cupboard which locked with a key. Will sustained a slight shock at the sight of a portrait on the wall. It was of a man some days dead, his flesh green and slashed open with swords, and maggots among it. It could still be seen that he must have been handsome.

"That is the man who maybe thought he could father my bairns," he heard the king say. "He was killed in the sea, a year since."

The Bonnie Earl. Will had heard the ballad sung earlier, at an inn in the Grassmarket, where a clarsach player had come in and gone his rounds. The tune was that of a dirge. Shakespeare remembered seeing a man in a slouch hat, seated alone at a table, listening. He himself hadn't waited long, being ready to bustle about as manager, down at the palace. Later he heard an echo of the dirge, under the windows of Holyrood. Either the king cared nothing, or else was afraid. Now, he was certain that what James felt was triumph. He had turned his back and was unlocking the cupboard. Presently he brought out a small oval object which opened on a hinge. It was a pleasanter sight than the dead young earl after eight days. Shakespeare looked down on the fair face of Mary Stuart, in youth as Dauphine of France.

He heard the king speak again. "What do they say o' me in England regarding my mother? Am I blamed for allowing her deith?"

How could he answer? He kept silence, and heard James continue as if he had not waited for any reply, knowing what it must be. "I kenned afore it," he was saying now. "A wise woman – there are aye such – came to me and said she'd seen Queen Mary's bloodied heid dance in the air. That was three days afore it happened, at Fotheringay."

He retrieved the portrait and again locked it away, as if still afraid the likes of his Calvinist tutors would chastise him for possessing it. "I was brocht up to think of her as a whore," he said. "I canna reca' her, though they say I screamed when her bright pomander swung towards me as I lay in my cradle, on what would be her last visit. She sent me a monkey in a gift frae her prison, and I loved the little ape and wrote to thank her for't. Jane Kennedy, her waiting-woman, who cam' here afterwards to marry Sir Andrew Melville and was drowned, poor soul, at the Queen's Ferry, told me my letter never reached her, and that she had sent many gifts and letters over the years, which didna reach me either. I doubt they are in Cecil's cabinet in London."

"Why would they prevent a child's letters reaching his mother?" He knew well enough; it was their suspicion of popery being allowed to influence the young king. With a mother who was thought by many to have a prior right to England over the existing queen, it would end by a return of England to the pope and, worse, the power of Spain, briefly wielded in the reign of the queen's dead half-sister, Mary Tudor. There had been burnings then, but nothing like the torments and executions before and since. James VI was outwitting them, taking a middle way as far as he might, being at the same time careful not to offend the old queen of England, whose heir he hoped to be.

As a child he would have known little of any such matter, being kept at his books. Will could remember the coin he'd handed the clarsach player; it bore the head of a thin-faced boy with swollen eyelids, and a closed crown the shape of St. Giles's steeple. George Buchanan's godly cane had kept the little king in order. He must continue to believe, or to appear to believe, that his mother had been a whore.

A wooden panel hung on the wall, so long there that James must have ceased to note it except in what remained of his child's inner mind. It had various painted figures and banners. A dead young man in armour lay on a bier, hands piously folded. An older couple, his parents the Lennoxes, knelt to the right, and in front of them was a plump infant wearing the same closed crown. The child James himself, portrayed further back in bed and praying, had words above him: 'Hear and avenge my cause, O Lord.' Two murdered men, in nightshirts, were shown lying in a garden, one with his long legs exposed as if dragged unwillingly along the ground. "Have pity on me, kinsmen, for the sake of Him who pitied all the world," Darnley's last cry, was not shown; nor was the other slogan current at the time, "Remember gentle Henry, and a vengeance on Mary." Will had heard some of that in England still; James Stuart would certainly have been told of it. He was speaking now, regarding the dead queen's likeness replaced in the cupboard.

"The world changed for me when Esmé came out of France, bringing that portrait and more. He was the first to tell me the truth about my mother the queen, and her innocence of my father's murder. He taught me about beauty and the sonorities of rhyme. I began to write poesy and wrote one – ye sall see it, Maister Shakespeare – begging the gods to grant me the gift o't, as they had done to my ancestor the first James Stewart, wha wrote *The Kingis Quair*. He was in prison, and so had I been, till then, without knowledge o't. Esmé helped me, he and Arran, to arrest Morton and have his ugly heid aff by means of his ain Maiden, his invention. He'd hidden from my grandfather when they were a' put to the horn, and leased himsel' to a farmer, and learnt about scythes and the like, wi' sharp edges. His ain invention in such ways cut his heid frae his neck by the end, and I was king.

"Then, Gowrie and the rest took haud o' me and shut me a year in a tower. I couldna win free till I'd signed Esmé's banishment. He died sune, back in France, and my heart was sair. Then Huntly set me free. For that reason I'm gratefu', and would cause him nae hairm."

The voice had sharpened; Will had the feeling that Huntly would not always have gratitude. It was a fleeting thought only; James had sat down at his table, and spread out the copies of the *Quair* with its verses of James I's love of Joan Beaufort, seen walking below in the Tower garden when he was a prisoner. They had married at last, had come home and had been most happy till the king's murder. For her protection, and that of their son the young king, Joan had married again. One of her descendants thereafter had been the Bonnie Earl. The other had been the third husband of Queen Margaret Tudor, possible father of Dorothea Gowrie.

He, William Shakespeare, had acquainted himself with every facet of Scottish history he could before coming here, knowing he would find inspiration in the tales he heard, and being anxious to align them with the truth as far as it could be done; for a play, one had to alter, but it was best to know what was being altered. One fact followed another in his mind now, as the king turned over the yellowed pages. *Tayis Bank* had been written by James IV to his love Margaret Drummond, who had died, they said of poison, the year before his English marriage; there was a tale, but he must tell it about other folk. Here was *The Jolly Beggar*, by the king's red-haired, lecherous and loveable grandfather James V, who being a half-Tudor could also be cruel when the mood took him. He had burned an innocent woman at the stake, and had hanged a Border reiver under truce. Yet *We'll ga na mair a-rovin' By the ae licht o' the mune* had been his, and he had been Queen Mary's father, dying when she was five days old. He had passed his poetry on to his unknown daughter, and she to her unknown son. There were many of James VI's own, and those of his father and mother. Darnley's love-poems to Mary were courtly, and seemed sincere. Mary's were mostly in Italian, a tongue she seemed to have found sympathetic.

"She had accomplishments," he heard her son say. "She was a notable embroideress. When I was a boy I foun' a handkerchief, sewn wi' strawberries in coloured silks. I didna ken whose it micht be, and I took it to my Lady Mar, who was my governess then, being the regent's wife. We a'feared her, but she was honest. She looked at it and said, "Never lose it, Jamie. The queen your mither stitched at it afore ye were born, waiting in Edinburgh. I mind her white fingers drawing, drawing at the silk." I didna ha'e muckle o' my mother's, all her gear having been ta'en. I kept it hidden about me, or else in cupboards, and looked at it often. I had it wi' me a' that year in the tower, after Esmé had told me the queen was no whore." He was staring down at his hands. "I never wash these, lest they grow red," he announced suddenly. "Whiles they cleanse the tips wi' rosewater.

"When I brought hame my ain queen, having made her mine in Norway, I had her crowned. She became it sae weel that I was pleased wi' her, and later gave her the handkerchief in gift. I didna say whence it came." His face darkened. "How was I to ken she'd be fule eneuch to gi'e my gift, the maist precious thing I had, to a capering long-legged loon wha pleased her in the dance? I didna hear o't at aince. When I asked her where it was she bit her lip, and said she didna ken. Then I get it out o' her. I was angry. I sent her from me. She's at Dunfermline nou, in charge of Sir Andrew Melville. He'll ha'e an eye to her, keep her frae ither folly."

Shakespeare felt a line come to him; *O blood, blood, blood!*

Later, it was as though the king forgot his confidences. He began to talk of other things, and grew jocose. "Ye maun visit the royal tombs ere leaving for the north," he said. "A few are there. They didna return my great-grandfather's body after Flodden, though his son asked for't."

Suddenly the too-big tongue, as a rule firmly kept behind compressed lips, protruded, wetting them. "Will ye read us *Lucrece* aloud afore leaving?" asked James VI, again sly and prurient. It was as though he was two different men. Then he reverted to his earlier self, the hooded eyes resentful. "Where the handkerchief is nou Huntly kens, for he killed the earl wha had it. He denies having seen it, but I doubt he's lying. The earl would keep it about him. Unless it went up in the flames at Donibristle, Huntly has it. He has maybe sent it to his countess at Strathbogie. When ye are there – I heard him ask – speir o' Henrietta hersel'. For love of me, she will gi'e it back. Do me this favour, William Shakespeare, and I will not forget."

Going out, a pleasant-faced young man named Willie Logie, who had been at the play, joined him. Will thought he might as well visit the royal tombs at once, while he was here; there would be small leisure later. He asked young Logie to direct him, and was taken to the chapel across the grass. On the way certain lines of the king's own poetry recurred to him. *When I perceive we marrows be.* From what had happened, it did not sound as if Anna of Denmark was her odd husband's marrow, merely a foolish and thoughtless young woman, occupied with trifles. As he had not yet set eyes on her, however, he could not judge. Certainly the king had been under strong and lonely emotion to have confided in himself, a stranger.

Shakespeare forgot it at sight of the tombs, ranged orderly in the half dark with no candles permitted. James V lay there, having died, they said, of a broken heart after a defeat said to be more shameful than that of Flodden. His first little bride, the king of France's daughter Madeleine, whom he had loved, lay nearby. Darnley's tomb was near, the recumbent effigy a copy of that on the wooden panel. It was unlikely he had ever worn armour in life. The queen in England had said she couldn't picture him with a sword in his hand, but that was unjust; he had held one at the coronation of Francis II and Mary.

Those tombs were close together. Solitary, before what had formerly been the altar, reared an older slab, unadorned by any figure or by words. Willie Logie laid his hand on it for instants.

"This is the tomb of Bruce's son," he said simply. "He was not thought worthy to lie beside his father and the earlier kings at Dunfermline. He made the mistake of growing too fond of the English, having been held hostage among them eleven years." He smiled at Will, adding that he and his sweetheart, Margaret Twinelace, who was at present with the queen, came here often. "A forebear of mine was his stepson, for he married a second time to the widow of Sir John Logie. Whatever folk say about him and her, he made a kind stepfather, and my forebear left a chantry for a mass to be said for the king's soul each twenty-second of February, which is King David II's death-day. It's past that now, because Father James Huntly was not here again till lately, which he is at present." He lowered his voice. "He will say mass for the dead early tomorrow, in Huntly House itself, because if we use candles here the Kirk will see them shining and come in and make a disturbance. I have confided in you, and I know you will keep the matter to yourself."

The information Shakespeare had sought had come to him without asking. It often happened if one waited in patience. He asked now at what time mass would be said, and where it was to be. It was to take place in the cellars, at half-past five tomorrow morning.

The man who played Grumio had drunk too much whisky. He had been intrigued with the peat-smoke flavour while at the same time faintly disliking it, but a local acquaintance made at the first inn had advised him to keep trying and he would accustom himself like other folk. Nobody here drank anything else, he was assured; ale was considered a woman's drink. Fired by these taunts, also by the secret fire in the whisky, Grumio tried and tried again. Shepherded by the acquaintance later on through various hostelries in the Grassmarket, the Netherbow and the Canongate itself, he found himself at last alone, unsteadily approaching two burning flambeaux in what was by then the dark. The flares appeared to waver and the saffron-shirted guards seemed to have multiplied. On asking one of them if this was not where Master Shakespeare lodged, finding his employer's name difficult to pronounce, a liveried personage came out and told him to take himself off. He was unable to do so, gave a sudden lurch and landed in the causeway. He was found there presently by Will, returning with his mind full of other things. The earl would not want such a guest. He picked Grumio up with some difficulty, asked him where he was lodging and could elicit no reply, and decided to take him round to the boys' Cowgate lodging; the widow there might be persuaded. Balancing the man's weight against himself he got him there, but it was still a district that thought a good deal of itself and when she opened the door, it was to say they didn't want that sort here. Will persuaded her with a silver coin bearing the crowned and sceptred Elizabeth; she looked at it with suspicion, while Grumio chose to be sick in the gutter.

"You English havena the wame for't." However this courteous balding man had met the king, and could charm her. She let them in and said the drunk fellow could share the young lads' bed. Will left this to happen, after half carrying Grumio upstairs lamenting that his head was in splinters and his purse had been taken. It was doubtful if he would be in a state to play tomorrow, and that left them short of a man.

It was late by then, almost morning; in a few hours there would be mass in the cellar. Will decided that it would be discourteous to disturb his bedfellows, whoever they were, and to take himself straight down. He brushed his clothes free of the smell of stale whisky, rolled up his short cloak and laid it at last under his head on a wooden bench, lying down for the time. It was still too dark to see more than a table which would serve as altar; the mass-gear would be with the priest.

It was dank and cold in the cellar, but Will must have slept on the hard bench. He was wakened by a warm glow of yellow light, coming from a taper held by the man in the slouch hat he had seen at the Grassmarket inn. He moved about quietly, lighting two candlesticks placed ready on what had been a bare table, now covered with a fair white cloth. He looked over as the other swung his legs to the floor.

"Sleep on, friend; it's early. You are John Shakespeare's son. My brother told me you were here. I am glad you have come down. Does your father fare well?"

His speech was dipped and precise, that of a man who has been brought up in France and speaks Scots as a second language. Will got to his feet, holding out his hand. He answered the question about his father, not troubling to wonder how Father Huntly knew. Jesuits were informed of everything, one reason why they were considered dangerous by the other side.

"Father, he fares better now he has nothing more they can take away. I have greetings for you no doubt from him, if he knew of it, but also from Father Colum, in Northumbria." That seemed a long time ago.

The priest smiled, and doused his taper. He resembled his brother the earl in certain features, but his own were disciplined by long training. "It is a pity old Colum did not continue his permitted time with us. It would have sharpened his wits, and they've gone. He preferred to return to serve his chosen saint."

"I made my confession to him, and I do not think I have sinned notably since. I hope I am worthy to be among you all shortly." He spoke humbly; it was so long since he had felt free to acknowledge his faith that it came as to a stranger. Father James Gordon – he used the Huntly name to distinguish himself from others – bowed.

"There will be plenty here for confession. If your conscience is clear, God will know."

"I have only resented one of my players who got drunk, and cannot work tonight or, maybe, come with us to the north the day after tomorrow. However I helped to find him a bed, and have left him the fare to join us or not, as he chooses."

"I may be glad myself of a place among your troupe. Disguise is useful, and the Kirk's commissioners will not look for a Jesuit among travelling players. I can learn a part quickly. I can play among you tonight in front of the king. He knows me in everyday guise, but give me a wig and a beard, and I will stoop like an old man or caper like a young one, and seem no longer myself."

He was preparing the mass-vessels as they talked, and presently others began to come down to the cellar, moving silently; the earl was among them, and young Logie. They celebrated mass to the memory of a man dead more than two centuries, a king shadowed by the legend of his famous father. Long abroad or in prison, with many ransomed years of a sterile and disliked reign, David Bruce's early promise as a young fighter on the Borders remained forgotten, as he himself did, in the minds of most. Yet he had made an able enough king, signing what he must sign, doing the best he might, unable to sire an heir through two marriages. That last had not been forgiven him, but the Stewart kings had followed from his dead half-sister.

At any rate, Will had his extra player. The Jesuit played with impudence that evening in *The Two Gentlemen of Verona*. Will himself would not have recognised Father Gordon had they met as he had now become. He set off, next day but one, with an added player in his troupe, making westwards instead of north as yet; they were to play for old Lord Paisley, and Grumio had rejoined them.

It proved to be a pointless journey all the way down to Paisley, except for Will's meeting with the old lord himself. For the first time, the sour-faced commissioners of the Kirk, who were stronger in the west, confronted his property-cart as it rattled over the stones, at last seeing the old abbey rise in the distance, and stopped its progress. Faces gaped out of it. Will, leading the horses, stood still.

"We will ha'e no ungodly players here. Ye maun turn back and mak' your way again whence ye cam'." He was asked to show pay-lists, and their passes out of England. It was noted there was one more on the list than the passes showed. Will remained suave; it was pointless to inflame these gentlemen, until lately paid by the government of the very land from which he had come.

Their round black caps and long black gowns, and their reverend beards, were an echo of John Knox himself, but they had not his fluency. Shakespeare pointed out that they were here not to perform in public, but by invitation of my lord in his own house.

"He is a papist and one of the Banished Lords. Also, ye ha'e a Jesuit in your company." But Father Gordon of Huntly had already vanished like the stars at dawn. Later he sent secret word to Will that he had gone to the south-west, towards Wigtown, and would ride to meet him again further north.

Lord Paisley, by then seated like Will before two sizeable stoups of wine in Place of Paisley itself, close up against the abbey walls as it had been since the beginning, grinned heedlessly above his growing paunch. He was undisturbed by the Kirk's officiousness. He himself was no longer as active as he had been in youth, but his spirits were still high. The players had been told to make towards Traquair, where they were anyway expected later. Enough had been made in Edinburgh to maintain them on their way. Will meantime had remained out of apology to the old lord, had been invited in, and asked instead to recite some of his verses; not *Lucrece*, on hearing which the former Lord Claud Hamilton had grimaced somewhat at court despite the gratification of the king. "Let me hear some of your sonnets," he said. "My forced sojourn in England caused me to ken somewhat of who writes there and what they jot down." He added that Father Huntly would be safe enough in Galloway. "He had a brither warded in Kirkcudbright for setting alight the House o'Towie, burning its lady and twenty-seven others inside," he confided. "They say a pretty lass fell out on the end of his spear, and Adam Gordon said she micht ha'e lived to be some man's delight, but he was a wild man, like maist o' his kin."

Shakespeare reflected that Kirkcudbright had once been dedicated to old Colum's saint, Northumbrian Cuthbert. In those times the borders had been different, and the saints had made their way north-east and south-west and up to Argyll. Later on St. Cuthbert had won the English two victories, one in the time of Stephen. He gazed in the ruby depths of his wine-stoup and began to recite, in his deep voice, such of the sonnets as he could remember. They brought back his depression, almost laid aside, over the dark lady.

Shall I compare thee to a summer's day?
Thou art more lovely and more temperate.

When he had finished that and others, Lord Paisley reached in his doublet and brought out a roll of fine cambric. "I keep this about me always, and it will be buried with me when I die," he said.

It proved to be a long tress of bright red-gold hair, the late queen's. "Eleven days she dwelt with me, and they were the proudest of my life," he said. Will asked if he might touch the hair. It was soft as silk. "Had old Argyll not fainted like a woman, we'd have prevailed against the bastard Moray at Langside. As it was she fled into England, and cut off her bonnie hair and put on a black wig lest she be known. They say it was grey lately, and shaven, when they severed her head. She had headaches in prison. They kept her in damp houses. She used to sew to pass the time. There is a tapestry of hers at Sheffield, maybe, or Tutbury, naming her son. *Unum solum, quid leonem.* I wouldna ca' James a lion myself, but she never knew him."

"A crouching lion, maybe," put in Shakespeare; a great cat, waiting for its mouse, claws sheathed. The men who had fought for his mother were of a different breed. It was said this old lord had had a hand in the murder of two of the regents; Moray himself, and the king's own grandfather, Lennox.

Lord Paisley had meantime put away the lock of hair in its wrapping. He heaved his bulk to the window.

"The Lord's messengers have gone," he said. "Come with me to see the abbey, and the grave of Bruce's daughter. Her son was the first Stewart king."

* * * *

Afterwards, riding to the west, Shakespeare wondered if there would be any end to the tales he was garnering and the uses to which they would be put. He had enough material already from this visit to keep him writing a year. He had been able to send money back to Stratford, to his father and Anne and the children. The Scots were avid for entertainment in their houses as a change from long war. Of their heroes, he had heard most mention of King Robert the Bruce, whose daughter Marjory lay in her tomb lately visited by him in Paisley Abbey. She had been returned after Bannockburn from eight years' prison in England, and married to Scotland's High Steward, who had fought well in the battle he, Will Shakespeare, had always been taught to look upon as England's great defeat. Perhaps heady with freedom, the Steward's wife had ridden out near her time, and her horse had stumbled and thrown her at a spot between Paisley and Renfrew, where she lived. So much my lord had told him; and the rest was legend. Her child had been torn alive from her dead body, and proved a son who later became Robert II after the death of Bruce's own late-born heir. "He suld be remembered for mair than siring over many sons by twa wives, for he was a fighter and saved the army at Durham when the young king was ta'en." He could still hear old Lord Paisley's voice. David II being childless, the man who had been Guardian of Scotland at last became its king "but he was auld then, and the sons fell out amang themselves. The best o' them was maybe the Wolf o' Badenoch. The sorriest became Robert III, wi' a sore in his leg so he couldna reign; but the Stewarts by then were kings, and Robert III's son was the first James Stewart, and wrote verse like your ain. His auld father died o' a broken heart when the boy was ta'en at sea by the English, and they kept him many years, but in the end he made a fine king, sae fine they murdered him."

The old lord would have kept him longer, but he had had to ride after his troupe. He found his mind arranging images in patterns, lines of verse. *Verse like your ain*. Lord Paisley had meant what he said; he was no man's flatterer. The compliment stirred Will to greater imaginings, the thought of the dead woman by the roadside founding a dynasty. *It cam' wi' a lass, and it will gang wi' a lass*; the dying James V had murmured on hearing of the birth of his daughter. Yet the crown was still on James VI's head. It was easy to picture strife for a crown, murder done to wear it. Some scene of triumph over an enemy, of victory against odds, would use a line which came to him now, recalling Marjory Bruce's death and the birth at the roadside in the dust, the birth of a king from a dead woman.

> *Know ye, this king was from his mother's womb*
> *Untimely ripp'd!*

The term 'this king' was wrong. It must be the name of a character in the play. The play could be about Scotland; a good king against a bad, some other man, a noble perhaps, fighting for the good, vanquishing the bad with that line. He hadn't yet worked out the story, or much else; only that recurring line. It would certainly be a separate play from the one bringing in the strawberry handkerchief. James VI had plucked at his sleeve on going, had reminded him again to be certain, when he reached Strathbogie, to ask about it, to find out from the young countess, Esmé's daughter, what had become of it. The king had been convinced that she would know. If she did not, he would have done his best. His mind was taken up with images. It was almost time to begin to write some of the notions down. Perhaps there would be leisure at Traquair.

The Shrew had also progressed; he added a few lines

inside his head while riding to the east. However he was beguiled by the beauty of the countryside through which he began to pass. Its greenness reminded him of his native Warwickshire, and the air here was no longer sharp. The trees, hills, brown rivers with pebbled reaches, and the occasional little fall of water, seemed like Arcadia. Who had said this was a wild and savage land? So intent was he on his surroundings that he hardly noticed a rider sidle up to him; the priest. He wore garb like a merchant, and was only recognisable by his voice.

"They helped me away early from Wigtown with clothes and money." Later he told Will the reason; for now, the Fleming lords were suspicious of anyone with French dealings. It was not long enough ago to be forgotten that one of their number, aged twenty-four, had been the third envoy to die of poison for refusing to take the Scottish regalia out of the country in order that the Dauphin, Queen Mary's first young husband, might be crowned with it in Paris. The other two had died at once; he had come home.

"Fortunately they are less likely to poison us at Traquair," said the Jesuit drily. Informed of the progress of *The Shrew*, and the possibility of putting her on there, he smiled a little. "It will be well received. They have a history of such women, and one of them ye will undoubtedly meet."

"Janet of Traquair?" That could not be, surely; Angus' handfast wife would be approaching a hundred years old.

"A different Janet. There are several." He added that Will would find a curious state of affairs at the famous old house. Brother had succeeded brother without heirs of their marriages, and the various widows lived on together. "The family itself sprang from a liaison, but the son of that fell at Flodden. It should not, therefore, be allowed to die out. I will be saying mass in the chapel for them, and will pray that there may be a son of the latest marriage. Do you do the like?"

Will agreed, realising how he was becoming accustomed to being quietly ordered. Father James Gordon had an authority which would one day make him Superior of his Paris branch of the Society of Jesus. Meantime, though there was the constant danger of prison for him, at Traquair there should be little danger of plague. Nor had there been any word of it in Edinburgh. He had been justified in coming, and the earl of Pembroke in sending him. So far all the players were well, even Grumio, and he himself was earning enough to pay them their wages punctually in addition to sending money home.

They came at last to the legendary house, towered, delicate and strong, pale in the sunlight that ended a fine day, its great breadth of scythed grass lying long and green before him. He had no means of knowing the Bonnie Earl had felt the same last year but one. To one side was the small chapel, undamaged in these remote parts. William Stewart himself came out of it to greet them. His hair had grown grey since the young earl's murder. Shakespeare was made known to a man full of care; my lord of Traquair explained that he had just been summoned to attend Parliament. It was a sign of the times that Gowrie's friend should be so.

The priest disappeared to hear confessions before mass next day. Meantime Will decided the evening was fine enough to try out *The Shrew* on the grass, where several of his players stood about. In process of arranging this he took time to gaze up at the fair towers, and wonder which of them had, in her time, contained wild Janet. He remembered hearing something of her from an old, old man who had been a page at Greenwich in Henry VIII's time. His memory was still clear enough to recall the brave Scotswoman who had come down to beard the king. She had worn her hair long and her gown loose, at a time when other women laced themselves and fancied stiff square fashions, and she had walked as if she were dancing. Maybe that was what had beguiled the young heir to the Angus earldom, on his way to do likewise with the widowed queen. He had no doubt had persuasion enough to gain the support of King Henry afterwards.

Will meantime saw the boy who was to be Katherina into her upholstered gown, and there was much laughter on the grass from players and spectators as they rehearsed. However at the end, a formidable dame in mourning, aged perhaps forty-five, approached Will.

"That play was written to mock me," she said. "I ken it weel eneuch. I am famed for my tongue, and ye sall hear it nou. Walk with me awhile on the grass."

Will was thirsty after directing the rehearsal, and must have looked it; many of the players had been brought ale. The widow had mercy on him, and beckoned a serving-man, who came back with two flagons. It was the best ale Shakespeare had ever drunk. "They brew it under the chapel," she told him, seeing his pleasure. "When the must rises we ca' it the odour o' sanctity. My name was Knox afore I was mairrit, and ye will ha'e heard of the famous Master John. He would ha'e managed your Shrew to her benefit."

"I heard he married a young girl of sixteen when his beard was grey." He had determined not to be mastered by this forceful lady, who must be the widow of whichever laird.

"He did that, and she was a Stewart forbye. They're a kenspeckle clan."

"My lady, I am an ignorant Englishman, and have not yet made myself at ease with your Scots language."

"Weel, ye could maybe say they staun' out in a crowd. She was an Ochiltree, kin to the deid young earl."

"Tell me of the earl," he said, anxious to get in a query, if possible, about the handkerchief.

"He cam' here not long afore," she conceded, then looked at Will with sharp eyes. "Ye ha'e seen the king, I hear. What for would ye be wanting news o' the puir young earl?"

He retreated; he would get nothing out of her. "It is only that I have a curious nature, by reason of my trade. Forgive me if I should not have asked."

"O, it's a' past. My gudeman, John Stewart that was, saw the knighting o' the king's feyther, that great gowk Darnley, that suld ne'er ha'e been mairrit tae the queen. I will tell ye a thing, Maister Shakespeare. Darnley was bastard get, as all ken at Traquair."

Will waited. He would not say whether he had heard it or not. "The king kens it, and that was why sweet Willie Gowrie lost his heid, for he had as strong a claim as ever Henry Darnley. He was mairrit forbye wi' Dorothea Stewart, Methven's dochter maybe by the auld queen."

"Why do you say maybe?" put in Will. "A father can be in doubt, but not a mother, surely."

"Well, it was Dorothea hersel' said it, and that she was the last to survive out o' mony. It had been the same when Queen Margaret was mairrit to James Four, God save his soul. They had six bairns, and only one lived to be James V at a year auld, God save him likewise. After she took up wi' Angus there was the ae dochter, the Lady Margaret Douglas, who lost six bairns out o' eight when she mairrit Lennox, and a pity Darnley was ane o' the twa that lived. Tudor blude has a badness in't, and our king has it himsel'."

"Queen Margaret divorced Angus, and married Henry Stewart, who was made Lord Methven by her son the king." He knew as much from England; old Henry VIII had called the third young husband Muffin, and disliked him. He was anxious to ascertain the real story of Dorothea, and guided the widow back to the point at issue. She was glad enough to talk about Queen Margaret Tudor, by now over fifty years dead. At first immensely welcomed as James IV's bride, she had been considered to betray his memory by remarrying so soon after Flodden. By the time of the third marriage and an attempted fourth, she was despised.

"O, she mairrit Methven, ca'ing him her dear Harry Stewart, in great haste afore her divorce cam' through frae Rome. She neednа ha'e fashed hersel'; the Angus marriage was nane, for he had been earlier united wi' our Janet, and they had a dochter a second Janet, wha mairrit Ruthven at last, for they had a hard time finding her a husband, the bruit having gane abroad that she was Angus' bastard, which she was not. It was the Lady Margaret was his bastard, and I say it nou as I'd ha'e said it then. Together she and Ruthven had William Gowrie, as the king made him after. In the meantime the auld queen had paid more than twa thousand pound to buy Traquair silence and gi'e Harry Stewart Traquair. Do ye ask why she'd fled back to her brother the king in England earlier, giving birth to the Lady Margaret Douglas in a peel-tower in the rain on the Border? It was because she'd fun' out about the marriage o' Angus and Janet, and kenned she hersel' was no wife."

Lord John Stewart's widow leaned closer to Will, even though they were safe on the grass. "I will tell ye mair," she said. "She'd to come back to Scotland in the end, for King Henry couldna long thole her girnings. She and Angus were like cat and dog for ten year, then the young king won free and put a' Douglases to the horn. The queen mairrit Methven, and he gave her bairns who died, unless Dorothea was ane at last who didna. He himsel' was a young man, and kept a lively mistress on one flair in Methven itsel', wi' the queen in anither, and baith o' them bare him bairns. After the auld queen died he mairrit Jenny, who'd had husbands afore, and made a' his family by whatever wife legitimate afore he died himsel'. If Dorothea says she was the queen's, there's naebody can tell either way; but the king heard it, and didna like it. Jenny hersel' went on to marry our second Janet's widower, auld Ruthven, wha helped kill Queen Mary's Italian Rizzio lang syne. His son, our Willie, was there as well. Later still Willie put the king in ward in Ruthven tower to rid Scotland o' Esmé Stuart, a Lennox come out o' France. Our king wouldna forgi'e that, for a' he gave Willie the Gowrie earldom; or the marriage to Dorothea, or that the bonnie earl was kin to him. They're a' Stewarts frae auld Hearty James, who was the son, one o' three, from Queen Joan Beaufort's second marriage wi' the Black Knight o' Lorn. The Beauforts were barred frae the English crown, but a Beaufort was mither to Henry the Seeventh, and he claimed it in her richt. Never ask who's bastard. He was Queen Margaret's father."

She went on from there to castigate the queen's brother Henry VIII for many reasons, also Darnley's father Lennox, Esmé Stuart's uncle, a renegade from the Scots Archers of the Guard of France. Old King Henry had allowed him to marry the Lady Margaret Douglas, by then over thirty and despairing of marriage, on condition that Lennox made war for England on the Border. "Muckle harm he did, hanging bairns wha were hostages. It was maybe a judgement that maist o' their ain died. Now here, Maister Shakespeare, is a strange thing ye may put in your plays if ye will. Huntly and Lord Claud, who had a finger in every pie, killed Lennox atween them when he was regent, after, when the king was six. Ruthven's brither was killed alongside Lennox. They carried in the dying regent wi' his guts hangin' out, and the young king saw him die. What kind o' a mon, having seen that, would befriend his grandsire's killers? Yet Lord Claud, Lord Paisley as he is nou, gaes free about court, and Huntly's close to the king, having freed James frae the tower and later, killed the bonnie earl. As for the Wizard Earl, it's a wonder he hasna been put to the horn." She meant Francis Bothwell, whom Will had not met, but who had been known to confront the king and threaten him, apart from the matter of the North Sea witches. "They say he's crazed," remarked the widow. "His mother's mairrit a third time, to a peaceable man." Will did his best by then to stem the flow, having heard enough. He wanted more ale.

"Well, the earl of Huntly's brother is here to shrive you, and will maybe have done the same for him." It was perhaps the wrong thing to have said to one born a Knox.

"God be thanked," she snapped, and walked away. Will was left with what the loquacious widow herself would have called a clamjamfrie in his head. It was next to impossible to straighten out all she had told him of marriage and no marriage, motive and murder and fell intent. All that seemed certain was that the king craved the crown of England and would go to any lengths to obtain it. His claim was through both his parents and Darnley's mother, the Lady Margaret Douglas, countess of Lennox, grandchild to Henry VII on whichever side of the blanket she had been conceived. Mary Stuart, legitimate grandchild of Margaret Tudor, that king's daughter, would have been unwelcome on her own account to half England as a papist; her son's claim rested hard on the father's side. To remove the rival earl of Gowrie on a thin excuse disguised Gowrie's double claim, and his wife's tongue was silenced by banishment. The stern and troubled laird who had been Gowrie's friend, and had walked by his side to the block, would know more; but he, a stranger, could not ask. What of the children of Gowrie's marriage to the mysterious Dorothea? They would perhaps be marked down for destruction. He remembered the two beautiful young men at court. *Vengeance to the third and fourth generation*, James Stuart would be capable of it.

At any rate *The Shrew* had gone off well. That was his concern, and not the other. He had no wish to end in a Scottish prison himself.

Will had decided not to put on *The Shrew* at Dunfermline for the queen. James VI had said she liked diversion, so *The Two Gentlemen* would again suffice. They got together their gear and once more rode north-east, leaving behind the fair Border landscape and the house of Traquair.

Coming to the Queen's Ferry, they were joined by a familiar face; Willie Logie, blithe at the prospect of Mistress Twinelace's company again. He handed Will a letter that had come for him after leaving Edinburgh. It bore Pembroke's seal.

He put it away till the turbulent Forth should be crossed, recalling how Jane Kennedy had drowned here, having fulfilled her destiny by telling King James the truth about his mother and how her ladies had greatly loved her, and had lamented at her execution. Jane had been newly married to Sir Andrew Melville, who was in charge of the queen now at Dunfermline. They came to the small town, where kings of Scots were buried from the time of Malcolm Céann Mór. He had married a Saxon princess who built the small chapel still permitted to stand, although the reformers had wrecked the interior and the graves. Queen Anna's new house however stood well-furnished; she had used the time since the earl's death to choose curtains and tapestries.

Will by then was beyond thoughts of Anna. His letter had conveyed sad news from England. His dear friend, quicksilver errant Marlowe, had been killed in a tavern brawl at Deptford in May, as they themselves were relishing the good ale at Traquair. Kit Marlowe had loved ale and life; had shared Will's spirit, had written certain things in common with him, including the play *Titus Andronicus* which was still unfit to be put on. He had had an uneven genius, which when it burned brightly more than equalled Shakespeare's own. London would be empty without him; but as Pembroke pointed out, there would be a vacant place left for Shakespeare to fill. He was not told to hurry back, as the plague still threatened; but it should be over once the summer had passed. He must return by Christmas.

Sir Andrew Melville himself greeted them at the door of the queen's new house. He was grave, being a widower, but Will thought he must have made an awe-inspiring bridegroom for his Jane. He was a prominent reformer, much older than she; and known for his lectures on theology, Hebrew, and several ancient languages. He was a travelled man and knew Paris, where he had been partly educated, becoming a professor at Geneva, Calvin's town, before returning as principal of Glasgow University. He had helped draw up the Presbyterian Second Book of Discipline, and had preached against absolute authority – the king's – before the General Assembly, of which he was often moderator. A better guardian could not have been found by the king for frivolous Anna. "Are you my keeper?" she was said to have asked, according to young Logie. Melville would know French, in which she was still more proficient than in Scots. Remembering the widow of Traquair and her baffling language, Will had sympathy.

He saw the young queen first from the improvised stage in the hall of her house, where many sat ready. She seemed sullen and pert, judging from her expression. Later, from Logie, he learned that it was because the king had sent for her to come to him at Falkland, royal place of the hunt. No doubt James, having made certain the Bonnie Earl had not fathered a bairn for him, had decided it was time to make his own.

Meantime Anna, pleased with the play by the end, clapped with her large white hands. By then Will had noted two beautiful young women seated near her; they greatly resembled the young earl of Gowrie he had seen at court, and later learned that they were two of his sisters, Barbara and Beatrix Ruthven. It was intriguing that the name was pronounced Riven. There was a fatal quality about all of the family, as though the sword that had killed Rizzio still hung above their heads.

They rested at Dunfermline for a day only, then made some haste to the north, the priest still with them. Will had told him of Marlowe's death and the reason for his own urgent return. "I will be glad of protection up to Sutherland," replied Father James Gordon firmly. He added that there was much to show Will on the way that would interest him and provide him with future plays. That, after all, was one reason why he had come. He scribbled a line to Pembroke in the light of a Fife summer evening, saying he would return soon, but meantime had promise of money. Even an earl would not despise that.

Before he left, an exquisite child, not more than ten years old, had come to Will with an invitation from the queen to be shown over her fine new house. The horses and cart were waiting, and the troupe, but it would be ungracious to refuse.

"What is your name, darling?" She was much older than Susanna, but had the same trusting ways. Susanna however would grow up plain. Will took delight in watching the lovely child as she guided him from one room as it opened on to the next, with everything polished and new, the hangings still garish with their woven patterns undimmed, framing soft beds with feather ticking. Either, he thought, the king did not stint his Annie of money, or else she had borrowed it. He thought of another queen, Margaret the Saxon, who had filled the little chapel not far off with brightly coloured tapestries and the great jewelled cross she had brought from Hungary. All, with the royal tombs, were gone.

"I am Margaret Stewart," the child had said; perhaps that had made him think of it. She added that her father and mother were both dead, and that the queen looked after her. She had a sister and brothers at Doune, but they were too young to come to court.

Doune. This was the Bonnie Earl's daughter. She would become a most beautiful woman. The earl's looks had not been lost. He remembered seeing the sad rendering of them after violent death, hung in the king's closet.

She led him into the last room, upstairs; and there sat the queen, her skirts spread and her hair on a frame. She embraced the little girl, who clung to her. "Well, Maister Shakespeare, what think ye of our house? Sadly, we will soon be leaving."

He had been thinking, in fact, that he would dearly love to do well enough in his profession to buy a house like it in Stratford, full of such comforts. It would not be of grey stone, but of dark-timbered plaster, and he, by then, would be as well thought of as ever John Shakespeare in the good days. It might happen. He saw Anna pull a ring from her finger, with a jewel in it, and extend it to him. He hesitated, fearing the king's wrath, and saw her mouth grow wry beneath the long nose. The unexpectedly dark eyes held acceptance of what life would bring her.

"Do not be afraid; it is my own, given me by my father the king before he died, about the time of my marriage. There is money awaiting you downstairs also. Your plays have given us pleasure; and after all what else is left in life?"

He had bowed, setting his lips to her hand. Afterwards he reflected that she was not such a fool as folk thought. She would maybe regret her impulsive gift of the handkerchief. He had not dared speak of it here, but would ask in the north when he might. He wondered what the king thought, if he yet knew, of her care for Moray's daughter, and if he would care to see Moray's features again about court. James VI had his strangenesses; maybe the sight would even bring him pleasure.

He had the chance to speak of James Stuart privately after they had visited several houses in Perthshire. It happened at Methven, the castle where old Queen Margaret Tudor had lived with her dear Harry, and Harry with his dear mistress, afterwards his wife. Those two had had a son who inherited the title, but he had let the place decay out of despair; he had dearly loved the Regent Lennox, and after his murder had grown weary of Scotland. He wanted to leave for France with its memories of Lennox, but was shot and killed in Edinburgh on the way. His son cared nothing for the place, and it was lived in now by the King's physician, Gilbert Moncrieff. He and Will sat talking while the priest, who had come also, was visiting a sick person nearby. The place smelt damp and neglected, with weeds sprouting between the outer stones. The physician was a plain man in a black skull-cap. He asked Will outright what he thought of the king.

"He is a man who has been unhappy as a child, and is marred from birth."

"It is more than that," said Moncrieff, who evidently wanted to talk about it and seldom found an audience who would understand him; this Englishman with the perceptive gaze would do so. "There is an illness which afflicted his mother, and his mother's father, and he has it also. It came to the Scots kings, I firmly believe, with the Tudor marriage; before that there were never deaths of as many children. I believe it also to have come from Queen Margaret Tudor's Plantagenet mother, and to go back in that line, for Joan Beaufort had only barren daughters by the king then, and a son at last, who luckily lived, but with a great birth-mark."

"What other forms does it take?" asked Will.

"At times a rash; the king has none, but his father Darnley had them, and it was blamed on the pox. Darnley's mother, besides losing many children, also had attacks of colicky pain, and in the end died of one; it was said Elizabeth's Leicester had poisoned her. There is always talk of poison. The old queen gave her a royal funeral. This illness varies; there are attacks of fainting, like Queen Mary had at Jedburgh when all thought her dead; and the pain in her left side she had, and the white skin that slides to the touch. Our king has it from his mother." Will remembered the dirty white hands. "His urine is a strange colour, like dark wine," added the physician. "I do not know if his parents, or his grandfather James Fift, who had changes in his moods that made him seem like two different men, or the auld queen here, had that. All I know is that the king has attacks of suspicion he needna, like the death of young Moray – all know he is the real killer – or the banishment of Lady Gowrie after the death of her lord on the block. None of it makes reason, and all is unreason."

The priest had come downstairs, saying the sick woman was better than she had been. "No doubt your visit, father, has cheered her," said the physician, who did not seem to be one of the Kirk's men. He saw them past the door which had seen Margaret Tudor's unwieldy coffin carried out half a century ago. Will said he was glad to have seen the castle after seeing the house and chapel at Dunfermline.

"Well, King Malcolm Céann Mór won his victory not far frae here, at Dunsinnan," said the physician. "He killed the good king Macbeth, who'd reigned seeventeen year after killing Malcolm's father, King Duncan. He would never ha'e done it, they say, but for an old rhyme that said Birnam, north-west o' here, must come to Dunsinnan before he could defeat Macbeth. Malcolm fulfilled the prophecy by carrying green boughs frae one to the other, a moving wall of men behind the branches. Malcolm married a saint, as ye will ken, Father Gordon."

"Much of whose work has been undone," replied the priest drily. They rode off, with Shakespeare retaining one more image; a moving wall of men behind green branches, and a king's murderer killed at last by his son.

He and the troupe, always with Father James among them, travelled north and north-west, playing in the Carse of Gowrie, Strathearn and the Drummond country. Word spread back and forth that the players were worth hearing, and their journeys often retraced their steps; on one occasion Will found himself in Perth, the ancient capital. Queen Joan had ceased to make it so after her husband's murder, Edinburgh Castle being more easily defended. However she had been brought back here to Perth after her own mysterious death, and laid beside James I in a fine tomb in the Charterhouse. Will made his way to what was left of that; the outer walls. This had been one of the first places to be attacked by reforming mobs, driven to destructive zeal by the fury of John Knox. All that was left was grey dust. The niche where the Mother of God's image had stood was empty. The marble tomb, with the queen's long plaits gilded as in life, he had heard, was gone.

He stood amid the nothingness that had once been

splendour, and it was as if James I the king-poet himself had sent word to him.

Dunsinnan was an awkward word. Suddenly, Shakespeare heard it transmuted in his mind to smooth iambics. *When Bírnam cáme to Dúnsináne*. Young Malcolm Céann Mór, with his army behind green boughs, slew his father's greying murderer, who for seventeen years had been a good king. That would not do. For a play to be successful, the good must be good and the bad, villainous. Macbeth could be inveigled by a bad queen. There was a model from his mother's tales in his boyhood; tales of the dark woman who had led King Henry VIII to destroy all he had formerly stood for, and after all of it had borne him only a second daughter, by now great Bess. It must by no means be evident that he, Shakespeare, was making use of her dead mother, Anne Boleyn. The play was still only taking shape, and not completely; something was still needed. He would give it time.

He came out into the sunlight of the street and found a young man standing there. He smiled, and Will remembered he had seen him before at court. "I am Gowrie," the boy said simply. "I was at the play at Holyrood, before the king. Will not ye come and dine? I am at hame in my ain house, though not for lang. I am on my way to Padua to study law there. I hear ye ha'e a new play where a bachelor comes there to seek a rich wife. I do not so, but I hope to aid my mother. The king took from her what he might."

Shakespeare was beginning to feel that the Ruthven tragedy pursued him wherever he might go, and he was nothing loth as such tales interested him; but by itself it was not compact enough to make a play, and as yet had no ending. He returned with the earl to a house he had already passed by, having at the time noted the coat of arms over the door, argent, three pallets gules, with supporters of a ram and sable goat, and below the motto *Deid Schaw*. He asked the young earl what it meant.

"Dry wood. We had lands in the north near a monastery, and gave the monks permission to take the dead wood for their fires. It does not mean we are dead wood ourselves. Come in, and have dinner."

Once inside he began to apologise for any neglect. "My mother may not live here to see to such a house, and my sisters, save the one who died, are at court with my next brother, and the rest at school. Your health, Maister Shakespeare, and many new plays from your pen."

Will refrained from staring openly at a second coat of arms over the fireplace. Despite what young Gowrie had said, it was newly painted and gilded, with a prominent difference from the one outside in the street. This inner shield had a coronet imposed, its bright gold shining out clearly.

The earl must have seen his initial glance, and raised his wine-cup. "Why should not our due be shown under our ain roof? My mother said, before she was made afraid, that she was the old Tudor queen's dochter. Papist claims may not obtain England for Mary Stuart's son. Philip of Spain's armada was defeated, but he is a man of strong purpose. He will never have forgotten ruling England for Mary Tudor. They say he would ha'a ta'en Bess hersel', but she wouldna ha'e him."

He was refilling his wine-cup too often, and talking indiscreetly. Will took heed of the warning about Spain; there were constant rumours of a second armada, with help from the Scots. Having met James VI, he doubted if his ambition included Philip II, but if there was a breath concerning fresh invasion, the Jesuits would suffer, and all Catholics, perhaps as was happening in England. He would warn Father James of what had been said, but would not see him for some days. He and the troupe were to perform at the old house of Stobhall, by request of one of the many Drummond sisters who had heard them elsewhere. Lord Drummond was a Kirk supporter.

Gowrie had begun to talk too much. "If my mother was wrang, and Jenny Atholl was hers and not the queen's, Methven legitimated a' his bairns by whichever mither when he mairrit Jenny. Methven himsel' had descent from Queen Joan and Edward III. That's as guid a richt to the crown o' England as any. Why, even Bothwell shouts to all who can hear that he's as much James V's grandson as the king. It's true; wild Jean Hepburn mairrit the third bastard John Stewart, and killed him wi' her tongue. Bothwell lately had his arms riven at Edinburgh Cross, and his wife went down on her knees to the king agin the attainder; but he'd asked for it for long eneugh, and the king has nae army to defend himsel' in face of suchlike visitors. Francis Bothwell's children are made beggars, accordingly, and so is he."

"What will he do now?" asked Will. "He is not in prison." The elder Bothwell had been chained there many years, in a Danish dungeon, till he died. It was small wonder he had first run mad, but this nephew of his, who pretended to order witches and no doubt fancied himself as the devil, was like Kit Marlowe, mad from birth. What, after all, was madness? It took many forms. He would write a play, perhaps more than one, about madmen. Londoners would pay to see such things; they found madhouses a diversion. In Scotland, it would not do. He thanked the earl for his dinner, wished him good fortune in Padua, and left. Maybe a study of the law would make the young man mind his own tongue, whether Jean Hepburn had minded hers or not.

At Stobhall, Lord Drummond the reformer paid him

unexpectedly well. This was all the better as my lord did not approve of mummers, as he called them. However his daughter Jean had written when she was with the queen at Dunfermline, and told her sisters to be sure to persuade their father. This seemed a tactful moment to put on *The Shrew*, and the old lord's grim face dissolved into laughter at the taming of Kate. It had taken place beneath the painted frieze of figures in the ancient hall, with broad Tay running not far off. Afterwards Lord Drummond told Will what he already knew, having seen the script in the king's Holyrood closet, of how James IV had written of himself as lovelorn, lying among the trees and flowers and watching the deer and wild things, and hearing the river run. There had come out among them *Natouris fair dochter discrete, the diamond of delyte*, Margaret Drummond, the young woman he had loved and wanted to marry. "My lords, though, would not permit it, there having been twa Drummond queens a'ready, ane o' them gude and the ither bad; a third would ha'e made our name possessed o' overmuch po'er. She died, they say o' poison, wi' her sisters, the year afore the English marriage. Margaret Tudor never had the king's heart. It was our auld lord aided the secret Angus marriage. A' ken the end o' that." He added what Will also knew already, that the daughter of the marriage, the Lady Margaret Douglas, had remained a firm papist in England after her father and the rest of his clan were put to the horn by James V. She had become a close friend of Queen Mary Tudor, and when the latter died and her half-sister Elizabeth gained the throne, Lady Margaret, by then Countess of Lennox, had sent her precious elder surviving son Darnley abroad to France, to be brought up by his Lennox uncle, Esmé Stuart's father. Shakespeare was glad of this information; it was one more piece in the puzzle. Young Darnley must have met Mary Stuart as Dauphine, when they were both young. Perhaps his mother, said to be a schemer, had known the Dauphin Francis to be delicate, and had foreseen a possible future. Certainly Darnley's verses to Queen Mary, which he had been shown by King James, had borne the possibly maternal refrain: *Be bowsome aye to knaw thy Lord and God*. Darnley had maybe not been the young monster now made out. James had shown him a letter in his possession saying how 'my love, the Queen' bore herself in all ways as a good and loving wife. That had been written to old Lennox near the end of the marriage, a year after the murder of Rizzio in which Darnley's part had certainly been treacherous. His Douglas kin, returned to Scotland, had pressed him to demand the Crown Matrimonial to increase their own power, then when he betrayed them and remained with Mary, they killed him.

Riding with the returned priest to Aldie, an old house in the Cleish hills where there were widows to be visited, Will thought of Margaret Tudor, the unloved queen. She had been handsome enough, they said, with her rose-petal skin and red-gold hair. Dunbar the friar-poet, who had come down to London for her betrothal and had admired that fine city so greatly he had called it the flower of all, had later written much verse in praise of James IV's queen, *the rose baith reid and white* from the marriage of her parents, the White Rose of York and the red one, hastily adopted, of Lancaster by Henry VII. After Flodden she was less kind to him, and his last poem said that *of leif nor flower, found I there nane of rue*.

He found Father James had been talking for some time about the Mercers of Aldie, so old a family that they were said to be older than Perth. They owned property scattered across the middle belt of Scotland, and had so much money they had lent it to the new Valois dynasty in France while at the same time, defying the English ships of Edward III with their own private fleet. "However there is a curse on heirs, and all ye will find this day there are widows, one a sick woman soon to die." It sounded like Traquair. Will wondered why there was a curse, but decided not to pester the Jesuit with questions. He would retreat into his silences, no doubt practising his spiritual exercises, then when he felt inclined would come out with some information or other as to what house, or what family, would be entertained by them next. Will had begun to feel that the matter was out of his hands, but the journeyings prospered, which was all he need care for. Yet he still amassed odd thoughts and lines, which came to him as they had done in the Charterhouse of Perth. The matter of the strawberry handkerchief continued to elude him, and he had accepted the need to bide his time.

Aldie itself proved to be a house with clustering turrets, having been made strong against attack. It was set high in the hills, small and intimate. The priest had already told Will a play would not be needed; he had called to console the sick widow, but the rest would maybe like a poem read. For that reason Will had brought with him a copy of *The Kingis Quair* he had picked up in Perth. The players, meantime, rested in their lodgings there before the progress northward tomorrow.

Will knew he had chosen the *Quair* because its gradations of feeling might be employed to suit a variety of company. The outspoken widow at Traquair could have been entertained with some of his own; *and in black ink my love shall still shine bright;* but here, one must wait and see. The sad prisoner James I of Scots had been gladdened by sudden love; but widows might not as readily be made glad. For some reason his mind flew back to the remembrance that one of the popes, who had their stupidities, had forbidden the playing of musical instruments by women in Spain, saying they must attend to their duties. However Queen

Mary Tudor, whose mother had been good Queen Catharine, had been taught to pay the guitar in the wild Spanish manner. He doubted if she had done so after King Philip had left her. There were those who died of a broken heart. His own seemed not to break.

The widow who greeted them would not be playing the guitar, or cards; she was ill. She was on her feet, however, to greet the priest, and smiled with discoloured lips. All of her flesh was yellow, even to the whites of her eyes. She was made known to him as Mistress Mercer of Meikleour, a great house some distance off to the east. It did not surprise him to learn that she had been a Ruthven before marriage. In Scotland women vaunted their maiden names and were often known by them through life.

"A thousand welcomes, Father Huntly. Ye will find us quiet here, as by custom."

The priest went upstairs with them to prepare for mass, for those who wanted to come. Shakespeare remained astonished by the freedom, despite the Kirk's ban, with which the old faith could still be practised in Scotland. South of the Border it would have meant, both for priests and those who sheltered them, an ugly death. Here, while the women and servants murmured their confessions in an adjoining room, it was possible to stand freely and gaze, from the high turret window, at a far loch glimmering blue-grey in the distance; Lochleven, where Mary Stuart had been tortured into signing her forced abdication and had then miscarried of Bothwell's twin sons. She had escaped, and scurrilous gossip had it that she had then borne a son to young George Douglas, who had helped her win free. It was lies, like many things one heard.

He made ready to serve as the priest entered, vested. The raising of the Host moved him profoundly, as always. They said – and this was maybe no lie – that Mary Stuart, on the scaffold, had had ready a consecrated wafer the pope had sent her, to be taken when in danger of death. It had been concealed in the blindfold she tied on for herself, then died with courage. She had exchanged her customary black sleeves for scarlet ones, in order not to show the blood. His own queen must go to bed each night with guilty dreams.

Afterwards they went down, where among those who had not come upstairs was another widow, her black hood hiding her face. She was in unrelieved mourning, somewhat shabby as if long worn. She was not made known to him, and after they had eaten a light meal, having fasted for the mass, Will was asked if he would read to the company. He brought out the *Quair*, having decided to cheer these sad women. The widow from Meikleour meantime spoke to him; "Ye may wonder why I'm here, and do not choose to die in my ain bed. I bide with my late husband's kin to be near a physician, both of the body and the soul. Do ye ken Robert Henryson's poem, Maister Shakespeare, where Cresseid turns into a leper? I had beauty ance, and 'tis gone."

"He made Cresseid loathsome, lady; you are not." Another notion, another tale; the handsome prince Troilus, son of Priam, riding past a huddled woman leper on the way, not knowing her for his lost and scornful beauty. *Troilus and Cressida*. His fingers itched to hold a pen; but he sat down among them by the fire, told them the story, which they would already know, of the boy James captured at sea by the English on the way to safety in France, and the news broke his old father's heart and killed him, so the boy became king. "He was a fine boy and we educated him well," he smiled, wooing them with his irresistible voice. "He became a poet, and while he was in prison in the Tower he heard the sound of jingling bells, went to the window and saw a fair young lady in all her jewels, walking below. At her feet was a little dog, with bells on its collar. The sight, he said, sent *The blude of all my body to my hert*. Later, when his ransom was paid by yourselves – the Scots had seen how well he was made to fight in France, and he made himself known to them – he and Joan Beaufort were married, and came home to Scotland. He had written a long poem about all of it, a part of which I will read you, if I may."

"It was her uncle the cardinal made her dress up in a' her jewels, to catch the king," came a voice. "He kenned weel eneuch the bells would bring ony man to the window. That airt got naething but barren dochters, save one that was a deaf-mute, and her line by twa husbands ended in the daft Mortons. By good fortune, Queen Joan had borne the king twin sons by then, wi' ane deid. She did better by her second man. By the time o' his trial, Morton's lady had been mad twenty-twa year, they say, and he maun ha'e kent it when he took her for her title. He got ten bairns on her, though they didna live except for twa spinsters naebody would tak' after the bad regent lost his heid, that still sits on the Tolbooth." Traquair did not have the only termagant.

"The princesses were maybe not all barren," put in Father Huntly. "One may be my great-grandam. It is said to be extremely difficult to decide who were the second earl of Huntly's children's mothers. Now let Maister Shakespeare read."

He did not, after that, read the passage about the king's first sight of Joan. He turned to the success of the marriage, showing that James I must have continued to write while ensuring, in a kingdom long rent by divisions, that the key kept the castle and the bracken-bush the cow. This had been his own words, and so were those that followed:

Unworthy, lo, but only of hir grace
In luvis yoke that easy is and sure.

In guerdon eke of all my luvis space
She hath me tak, hir humble creature,
And thus befell my blisful aventure
In youth, of love, that now from day to day
Floureth aye new.

There was a sound of sobbing. The shabbily clad widow he did not know had risen, tears coursing down her face. She turned and went out of the hall. "Dorothea, do not go," cried the sick Mistress Mercer. "He meant nae hairm."

The termagant turned to him. "Pay no heed," she said. "Lady Gowrie has had her sorrows. So ha'e we a'. Read on, maister. Poesy is glaikit stuff. Queen Joan got hersel' a lusty young gallant when her king was slain, and bore him three sons."

The sick woman put her hand on Will's arm. "Forget Queen Joan," she said. "Presently, go to Dorothea Gowrie; you, rather than the priest, can maybe comfort her. She was alone at Dirleton when the laird o' Traquair brought news o' her lord's death, and she blames her tongue for't. You will think o' the richt words."

He had not comforted Dorothea Gowrie, because nothing now would. She had heard his apology dully, as if it concerned someone else. Suddenly, Will had thought of a means of diverting her mind.

"Never blame yourself; such things were foretold already, before the king's birth. Your lord and his father, Lord Ruthven, were at the murder of Rizzio. James sees himself as flawed by reason of their sword-hilts while he was still in the womb. Later, as you know, your lord helped to clap him in the tower a year. All that would not be forgiven, and James used the tale about taking Stirling for your sake to kill Lord Gowrie. He had long intended it, maybe for most of his life. He took a like revenge on the earl of Moray, for being apt in the dance with his queen."

She had looked, at last, as though she saw him; he wondered if she resembled whichever woman had been her mother. "Think of the happiness your loves brought," he said. "That he cannot take away. I have seen your handsome sons and your lovesome daughters." He felt his own persuasion begin to fail; she had withdrawn again.

"He will have vengeance on them likewise," she said. "He will never rest till all of us are gane."

After leaving Aldie Will wanted to forget his blunder with Dorothea Gowrie; he felt any lack of sensitivity acutely. He made himself ask the priest about his royal or other ancestress without wanting to know more; the entanglements of Scottish descent seemed impossible to unravel. Nor did Father Huntly try.

"The second earl, while still Master, was short of money, and seized the widow of the Douglas, whose lord's head had been sent, they say, twenty-one days before to King James II. The Master craved her person less than her tocher and the broad braes o' Moray, also the fine house the Douglas had newly completed, at Darnaway. He mairrit her forcibly, but not long after saw a better chance: The Princess Annabella, the king's youngest sister, had been sent hame by the king o' France for barrenness through eleven years as the wife of the count o' Geneva. There had been the barren Dauphine and a barren archduchess as well, and Charles VII sent a large sum of money wi' Annabella in compensation, not being anxious to lose the alliance with Scotland. Huntly seized his chance and the princess, saying his first wife was related through consanguinity. It was often a convenient excuse."

"Did the first wife repine?" Will asked.

"By no means; she married again, to a Colquhoun. She had had heirs to the Douglas, but it's uncertain whether or no she bore ony to Huntly, or whether the princess did. After some years Huntly fell in love. This time, the Hays were an auld family, descended frae auld Robert II. King Blearie as they ca'd him, having weak eyes maybe from being born amang the roadside dust. Before that, the Hays took their descent frae the auldest kings of a', before the Stewarts cam' or the Bruces or Baliols, or Malcolm Céann Mór. Elizabeth Hay was of the blood o' Bethoc, dochter to auld Malcolm II, who died at Glamis aged more than eighty, having got Lothian from you English by a battle he won at Carham. They ca' it the Cession."

A rare grin crept over the austere face. Will could glimpse the Gordon boy this priest had once been, at home among his wild brothers, as swift with words as blows.

"Ye sall see the room where the auld king died, maybe, when we visit Glamis. Meantime the second earl, as he was by then, played the same trick wi' the princess he'd done wi' the first wife, saying they were baith related to each other and himsel'. After five years he was allowed to wed Bess Hay, and she bore him children, but whether some were the second wife's or the first's, or Bess Hay's, was never certain; they were a' brocht up thegither at Strathbogie wi' Huntly's bastards, some o' whom had the same Christian names as some o' the rest."

"It sounds a happy enough arrangement." It did not seem difficult to be descended from the Bruce's grandson. Robert II had had thirteen children by two wives, and nine more on the wrong side of the blanket. It was still talked of. The sons of the second wife, who had been noble, made war now and again on those of the first, who had merely been beautiful. Father Huntly spoke now of the Pembroke connection with Lady Katherine Gordon, the second earl's daughter whom James IV had given as a royal bride, one way or the other, to the young man who had come last century to Scotland claiming to be Richard of York.

"He may have been so indeed, but Henry VII was swift to do away with his Yorkist claims and, by the end, with him."

Shakespeare pointed out that after that cunning king's death, Lady Katherine had remarried three times, but never with children. "The barrenness would seem that she was the princess's daughter."

"If that is so, then maybe so are the folk of Gight," said the priest, who today seemed confiding. "The first laird fell at Flodden."

So many had done that; up here, it was a badge of honour. He was learning many things by having come to Scotland.

They went stravaiging eastwards, sometimes doubling on their tracks if a town or a great house sent word to them to come and play. Now that the weather allowed, on fine days they would play in the open, with the young boys going round afterwards cap in hand. One had grown taller and was beginning to have to shave; it showed how time passed. Folk were glad to be diverted, but the Kirk cast a cold eye, and even travelling on the Sabbath was frowned on.

In St. Andrews they did not play at all, as a conventicle of black-clad Geneva divines would not permit. The snell air still held the sensation of ashes and revenge, the burning of a young reformer, the grotesque murder of a cardinal. Nonetheless some of the older folk could recall the glitter of old days; beyond the fires that had destroyed George Wishart there was a memory of others, bonfires of rejoicing at the birth of a fine prince to King James V's new French queen. She could be remembered as well, riding through the town the day after her wedding to the king, a tall young widow as she had been, long-necked. They said the old king of England had wanted to many her, as he was so big he needed a big wife. "But my neck is small," Marie de Guise had replied, and despite the English ships had reached Balcomie safely, and married their king with splendour in the abbey here, which still reared at the end of the street.

That prince had died, nobody knew why; and his baby brother, born a year later, had died at the same time. Then the loveable, wayward king himself had died, leaving a daughter five days old to become queen of Scots.

Will knew the rest, having passed the charred skeletons of abbeys on the Border. Old King Henry had heard from his visiting envoy what a fine child the little queen was, and wanted her as a bride for his late-got son. The Scots would have none of it, and Henry VIII had sent armies with fire and sword; it was still known as the Rough Wooing. In the end the child's mother had had her sent secretly to France, to be brought up there and then married to the young Dauphin. Not all of the Scots were agreed on that; and by then the new doctrines were being spread, partly by the tongue of Knox, partly by the gold of England. Finally the Queen Regent had brought in French troops, and French troops brought the pox. Will and the players saw many noseless folk, limping or staggering about the ways. It had mattered nothing to them that the queen of Scots was queen of France, but that did not last long; at the death of her husband and her mother, she had come home, to an Edinburgh haar, the cold yellow fog that greeted arrivals by sea. That had begun her reign, and there were other troubles by way of her half-brother Moray, whom she trusted but who had wanted to become king himself. There had been the marriage to the long lad, Darnley, and the Rizzio murder and then Darnley's own. After the birth of the prince his mother had been abducted by Bothwell, who got himself a divorce from his new wife, Lady Jean Gordon. She was the priest's sister, and Will asked little of it. The queen and Bothwell had been married, she in black "but she wore black for the marriage to Darnley as well." That was Father James's comment, as they rode west again and then, having played in the towns, left them for the north parts.

"The queen and Bothwell had faced an army of my lords with one of their own at Carberry Hill. He had done well enough in raising men, and maybe would have won the day, but to save the shedding of blood they agreed to part, my lords having promised to treat the queen well. He rode off, and she returned with my lords to Edinburgh; but the crowds there had been stirred up against her, and called out on her for a whore, jostling her as she rode by. They lodged her that night in great discomfort, then took her to Lochleven, where Moray's mother was her gaoler. My lords came there and forced her to abdicate in the name of her son. She claimed after it that a forced abdication means nothing, as a forced promise means nothing. She escaped on the second occasion, having been brought back on the first; and raised an army with the help of Lord Claud Hamilton and others, but Moray defeated them at Langside. She would not again face the Edinburgh crowd, who would have torn her in pieces; and fled instead to her cousin of England, who kept her prisoner eighteen years, then executed her.

"As for Bothwell, he had been trying to raise aid in the far north, where his mother's folk were. He was driven by adverse winds to the coast of Norway, and there evil luck came to him. A woman who'd been his mistress here and in France, and was an admiral's daughter up there, said he had promised her marriage, and owed her money. By the time that had been enquired into, events in Scotland were known in Denmark, where Anna Throndssön's father was in employ. Bothwell was detained, at first in civility, later in filth. His dying confession absolved the queen of Darnley's murder, to the wrath of your queen."

There was no doubt, however, that Mary, Queen of Scots, bitter with betrayal, had plotted the death of the Tudor queen more than once. Will could remember the joy-bells ringing out in London at news of her execution after trial at Fotheringay. She had worn, he recalled again, red sleeves to walk to the scaffold, herself lame from years in damp houses in England. The red, she had hoped, would disguise the blood.

"We take the north road now," said Father James Gordon.

As they rode northwards the land grew less lush, the mountains made the English marvel, and the air grew colder. Suddenly, at a fork in the path, a clamour came, led by a daredevil with sword drawn, waving it and shouting; he was followed by a body of horse. The smell of their sweat, of the dust of long hard riding, came. The little troupe huddled at the side of the road, watching the horsemen sweep by. Their speed and the clatter of hooves, and the shouting, seemed aimless, as did the direction they took to the south. "It is Bothwell's nephew, the Wizard Earl," remarked the priest drily. He himself was as usual dressed like the others, in shabby travelling gear, his pack safe in the saddle. Francis Bothwell had not noted him, would never note anyone much except himself. As he galloped off into the distance, his minions behind him, Shakespeare was reminded of Herne the Hunter, driven forever by the devil, without rest.

"He will ha'e been to the north, to try for money frae his late grandam auld Countess Agnes's estate, for she left a' to his mither," said Father James, who appeared informed of everything. "He will maybe trouble the king again, or else not. Like enough we will meet him gaun back again the gait he cam'."

He had more to say about Bothwell's errant nephew, who should have been born with a silver spoon in his mouth, being Queen Mary's godson and named by her for her dead young first husband, briefly Francis II of France. "On the day of her marriage wi' Bothwell she wrote to the pope to ask for the abbacy o' Kelso for this bairn," said Father James. "She gie'd him Badenoch, which didna please Huntly, and on our getting it back again she saw to it that young Francis got Morton's forfeited rents. She was fond of him not only for Bothwell's sake but for that o' her half-brother John Stewart, his father. James V had provided her with much kin."

"I heard that when she was in prison in England, she wrote to ask that he receive the Bothwell title and estates, his uncle being dead." Shakespeare thought he must have heard of that from Pembroke, who kept in touch with events.

"That is so," said the priest. "His friendship with the young earl of Moray was perhaps his undoing, for with Moray's killing he grew angry and wild. It was about then the witchcraft matter arose, and Bothwell was imprisoned and escaped. He was forfeit within four days, and after Christmas twa-year since, shortly before the killing, tried to seize the king's person at Holyrood. It is a sign of the slowness of parliaments that it was not till now his arms were riven at the town cross. He tried again to seize the king at Falkland shortly after. James has no guards; the Scots Archers o' the Guard keep watch over the king o' France, never the king o' Scotland.

"The earl was not done then. This very summer he forced himself into the presence, and knelt before James with a bared sword. The king fears naked steel frae afore his birth, with reason; but when he tried to escape into the queen's chamber, the door was barred. It's feared she favours Bothwell by reason of his friendship wi' Moray."

"Is the king safe?" asked Will. He remembered the weak-legged figure, which had not held back from crossing dangerous seas to fetch his bride. It was sad if the bride betrayed him; but maybe she had bolted her door out of caution.

"He held his ground then, and said he was a king. He made promises, which my lords at Stirling later absolved him from keeping as they had been obtained by force. I doubt Bothwell may be heard of again, ever the more wild and with less hope. He may make some show of resistance, but he has naught left to pay an army. In the end, it may be with him as with his uncle, chained and mad. His best course would be to take himself abroad."

"But not to Denmark."

"Well, the queen's brother reigns there now; he might have a better fate."

Will lay in his lodging that night and did not dream, for he seldom did. He had kept before his waking eye the galloping horses, the mad leader intent on his own destruction and that of his children. The Hepburn blood had harmed, in its time, four queens. There had been that whisper that Queen Anna herself had been Bothwell's friend, and had barred her door against the king when he fled from that kneeling presence with its bared sword. James in the end had turned at bay and said, "I am a king." The witch Annis Sampson had said he was *un homme de Dieu*. Maybe that strength had prevailed.

Shakespeare turned in his half-sleep. It seemed now that the riders he saw were Francis Bothwell's own witches, those he believed himself to have sent across the sea in sieves to spoil the king's marriage. Not all were haggard crones; one was Francis Bothwell's mistress Barbara Napier, who had had her life spared while the rest burned. Shakespeare could not see her face. Her hair flung out behind her, streaming as they went.

Later he must have slept, because he awoke with a vision of three women, like Paris with the golden apple. One was young Barbara, one was Annis Simpson, who had been strangled out of mercy; and the third he could not name.

Three witches on a moor. He still had not completed the story in his head. There was more to be told, and they had not yet reached Strathbogie.

They came to Murray country, and the old castle of Blair, which was about to be rebuilt now such habits were the fashion. Will had been fascinated by the tongue-twisting names they passed by; Monzievaird, Aberlednoch, Balquhidder. They played meantime to the company within the stripped and echoing walls. A dowager, terrifying as an army with banners, sat in pride of place; she was old Lady Mar, who had been born a Murray and had been the young king's guardian in childhood and greatly feared by him; he had called her Lady Minny. She announced, with pride, to the assembly that the queen was with child. The birth was to be expected in February coming, and the king had removed his wife to Stirling Castle, where he himself had been christened with great ceremony and the refusal of the English envoy to enter at the door. "It was a papist affair, and Lady Argyll had to stand on the stool o' repentance afore the Kirk for being the royal bairn's sponsor," announced Lady Minny, a firm Protestant. As was customary in such instances, the priest was nowhere to be seen. "Yon Darnley wouldna be present, though the queen had got him a suit o' cloth o' gold," the dowager continued.

“That did her and the bairn muckle hairm, for it began to be said Darnley wasna the feyther. The good Lord will maybe send a healthy heir, to down such rumours if they still exist.”

She turned her head, on its high frame, to glare at a personable woman, Lord Tullibardine’s daughter Anna, no longer as young as all that, who was about to be married at last. There had been some hesitation from possible husbands, as the king was believed to have been taught to forget Esmé for the time by “fair Mistress Anna Murrey, the kingis mistress” during the year’s durance at the place he now caused to be called Huntingtower. It was even possible that some of the verses sent overseas to the other Anna had in the first place been written for this namesake, but that must never be mentioned.

Murray legends were diverse; old Lady Atholl, now dead, had had the power of incantation and was said to have cast Queen Mary’s labour pains on to Lady Rires of Wemyss in the small chamber in Edinburgh Castle in which the king had been born. However the queen had suffered so greatly that she had said she wished she had never been married. All this was talked about as if it had happened yesterday; and Queen Mary’s Bothwell, whom nobody ever remembered to call the duke of Orkney, had been challenged to a duel at Carberry Hill by two of the older Murray brothers present, but had declined both because of their lack of rank.

“The late Sir William chased him then on the high seas, and was present when my lords opened the casket said to contain letters frae the queen, saying she’d follow Bothwell through the world in a white petticoat. It may be she would ha’e done, but the letters were false; they’d changed the dates in the copies.”

After that Sir William had gone over to the queen’s side and had aided her escape from Lochleven.

Later the dowager sent for Will. “Ye ha’e an apt muse,”

she said. "Ye will ken my late lord o' Mar was the sole regent to die in his bed amang them a'. There was a daft tale that the bairn born to the queen was deid, and was hidden in the wa', and ane of my ain put in his place. They may look at a portrait o' my lord to make blethers o' that, forbye I mysel' ken when I gave birth and when I didna. I ha'e but the twa bairns o' my marriage; Jocky o' Slaitis, as the king ca's Mar, for your English lugs will not jalouse that to slait a carle means to beat him at the schule, and Jock did that aince to the king, scholar as James is by nature, forbye Maister Buchanan being owre gleg wi' his cane. Then there is Mary my dochter, who is my leddy o' Angus, and nae ither. Why, they say the king resembles my lord, but my lord was dark, like a' the Erskines. He was liker the Regent Moray, his kinsman. There's trouble eneuch without folk thinking o' mair o't. How did ye leave matters in England, Maister Shakespeare? There seems less fash than there was."

Will nevertheless knew they had to have particular care here. The priest was guarding the property-cart, his hat pulled over his eyes. Sir John Murray was one of the commissioners appointed by the Kirk to hunt down Catholics, as the Bonnie Earl had been expected to do in his day. There would commonly be a burst of arrests to maintain the commissioner's honour and his payment; then nothing more for a while, and presently a quiet freeing by the king of those in prison.

However prison is never agreeable, the less so when there is a task left undone. Will was thankful when they trundled away from Blair, with its building-blocks ready to form new towers.

He wished the absent queen well in her forthcoming labour. A prince would content everyone.

* * * *

"Ye will be grieved to hear o' the death o' Mistress Mercer doun at Aldie," said the priest, who had rejoined them once Blair was left behind. "I am saying a mass for her; come an ye will. The morn I ride to Glamis, to a sad woman there. If ye were to accompany me, ye may see the chamber where auld Malcolm II died at over eighty, that I told ye of, and there is more to tell o' Glamis."

Will attended Mistress Mercer's dead-mass and lit a candle, remembering her yellowed eyes. She had not had long to live and had known it. Dorothea Gowrie had lost one more friend; but she had twelve children still living, and many kinsfolk about Perth.

Meantime, after Blair, he again paid the players well, and told them to rest or else disport themselves for a day. "Do not get yourselves a rowdy reputation," he cautioned them, recalling Grumio's taste for whisky. They understood by now that the journey home would be met by means of further invitations to great houses; they had become a loyal and hard-working troupe. He would report to the earl of Pembroke accordingly, by Christmas at latest. The snows up here would in any case make travel uncertain by then. Meanwhile he rode off with Father James.

It was a long ride through the glens. The priest by now assumed it safe to take his own identity; he read his breviary openly in the saddle, leaving his horse to find the way. There was only the one trodden path. Shakespeare, not breaking the silence, felt his own thoughts burgeon. Lines rose in him from the earlier plot he had partly sketched out, regarding the man uncertain of himself, the husband demanding that his wife show the strawberry handkerchief of his gift. The wife was innocent, but someone, a villain to be developed, had put it into the husband's head that all was not as it seemed. The villain would be most persuasive if he were a man who seemed bluff and honest. Honest, honest . . . James.

The Spanish for James was lago. Later, the husband, disillusioned:

All my fond love thus do I blow to heav'n:
'Tis gone.

Could love die as easily? He had not taken leisure to think of his own for long enough. As the green glens widened towards the eastern plain, he made himself embroider the embroidery.

That handkerchief
Did an Egyptian to my mother give . . .
'Tis true there's magic in the web of it;
A sibyl, that had number'd in the world
The sun to course two hundred compasses,
In her prophetic fury sewed the work;
The worms were hallow'd that did breed the silk,
And it was dy'd in mummy which the skilful
Conserv'd of maidens' hearts.

His own thoughts were becoming wild and macabre, like Kit at his best, while the priest still read his breviary. He himself was thinking not of God but of witches, sibyls, evil. The murderer of a king had been a better man than the king he murdered. That must change. The murdered king must be gracious, reverend, old. The real Duncan had been young, and not distinguished. The audience would prefer Macbeth.

"I maun tell ye the tale o' Glamis," said the priest, putting away his breviary. He had less caution about meeting commissioners in these remote parts; there were too few folk to arrest.

It was sad and terrible enough. King James V, son of Margaret Tudor, in an access of grief and anger at the death from consumption of his young bride Madeleine, had accused an innocent woman, Lady Glamis, of trying to poison him. Although a jury declared her innocent he had had her burned publicly at the stake. "It was because she was a Douglas born, Angus' sister; and the king had sworn to destroy all of the name. Angus had made him a bad stepfather and the queen a bad husband, but his sister was in no way to blame. She maybe helped her kin when the king had put them to the horn. She died most bravely on the Castle Hill of Edinburgh, with the crowd crying out in pity. Her daughter Margaret lives on alane at Glamis. She was a young girl when her mother died, and now is old, but lives on. She has never mairrit, nor can she think of anything but that unjust burning, sixty year ago it maun be by now; she's a trifle crazed, as such folk become. The king got little gude o't, though he took possession o' Glamis, which is a maist fair place, hunting there often."

"Has she no kin?" asked Will in pity.

"Her brother is elsewhere on the king's business, and does not trouble with her. Do not, by the way, name Huntly to Margaret Lyon when ye meet. A former earl of ours had her sister's husband brought to the block for treason, and the Forbeses and the Huntlys are at feud still."

"There seem many feuds in your country."

"There were as mony in your ain, afore the Tudors put paid by making the causes shorter by a heid."

They had ridden far enough at last to behold Glamis behind the trees; a fairylike mass of towers wrapped in a high containing wall. Inside there proved to be little left, James V having helped himself long ago. The great hall was bare, and a shaft of lingering sunlight struck on naked flagstones. Down the turret stairs had already come, hearing their arrival, an old woman. Her face was white, like uprisen dough, as though she never saw full sun or light of day. She wore rusty mourning, with a long black veil descending from her coif.

"Ye ha'e come here ance mair," she said, as though the priest had no name. Perhaps she did not know it. Father Huntly said a few words to comfort her before taking out the flat pyx from his clothing. Shakespeare did not come forward, remaining in the shadows by the doorway, while the sun still outlined, with dusty motes, the two black-clad figures, the old woman and the priest.

"Nothing will console me now," said Margaret Lyon flatly. She stared at the Host between his thumb and finger.

"This that I ha'e brocht consoles all humanity. Your mother is with God, Margaret. Take heed to your own soul. Recite a prayer with me."

"The red-haired king is not with God. He is with the devil in hell. He burns as he made my mother burn, but for him it will not cease. When she died I cursed him and his heirs. They ha'e had small luck thereafter."

"Who are you to curse or to bless? You are furrowed wi' hate like dried-up leather. James V is deid, may his soul rest, and is maybe past purgatory. Do not speak ill o' the deid, Margaret. The fair young queen his dochter is deid forbye, and had cruel fortune; surely ye may pray for her soul?"

"I pray for my mother's, nicht and day. James V died o' a broken heart, they say. I say he had nae heart to brak. After my mother's burning in the fire he rode here year after year for the hunt, and I would not look on his face. He took away the twelve great silver flagons o' Glamis to melt doun for his coin. He took other things. He took my life. I'd stay up in my attic while he sojourned here, pleasuring himsel', but never wi' me." She was twisting her hands in a curious gesture, as if she constantly washed them clean. "I cursed him," she said again. "He had nae luck thereafter. My mother was bonnie, and never said a harsh word to ony. He burnt her, kenning weel she was innocent." Tears had begun to run down the white face. It was unlined, as though she lacked other experience.

"Will ye take the sacrament, Margaret? If so ye maun kneel."

"I kneel to no man, and no king. The king burned my mother. He burned her, I say."

"Have ye eaten in the past hour? If so, I cannot give ye the bread of God."

"How do I ken? They bring platters and tak' them away again. I neither see them come nor go. Who is this man?" The mad eyes had seen Shakespeare. Father Huntly kept trying to persuade her, like a child. Finally she took the sacrament, kneeling. Will, who had not eaten either, received it also. He was glad of it; it salved the memory of evil here, the persistent madness. The priest said to her Will wrote plays, and would like to see the room where the old king had died. Margaret Lyon grinned suddenly, showing darkened teeth.

"Never write a play about Glamis. What happened here is played out."

Will went up the turret stairs, having been directed. The small room seemed humble to have housed a king, a king so old. *Who would have thought the old man had so much blood in him?*

An old, murdered king. That was better theatre. An ambitious woman had persuaded her husband to murder, then could not stop washing her hands to be free of the blood. Anne Boleyn, in the Tower, had run mad with remorse. They had roasted Queen Catharine's confessor over a slow fire, and laughed, preaching over him at Paul's Cross. It must have been difficult to forget. *Can'st thou not minister to a mind diseas'd, pluck from the memory a rooted sorrow?* As for the murderer himself, he might not sleep.

Macbeth shall sleep no more.

It was coming. He turned and left the little room where Malcolm II had died, and went down again, finding the priest ready to go. "I will come to ye again, Margaret," Father Huntly said.

They left her staring after them, not seeing them. She turned presently and went back into the emptied hall. She didn't want anyone but her mother. She would live to be ninety-one years old.

The troupe would make its way to Cawdor, then Strathbogie. Besides delays on the way, Will had to arrange ahead, as had been the case from the beginning. At times, as at Paisley, they had had to retrace their steps because of a demand from some great house which had heard of them from the last; new lines had to be written, new parts created, costumes mended that were worn or torn, wigs teased, headdresses goffered when there was a fire to heat the irons at an inn, or a willing servant to do it for little enough. Up here they expected less than in the south, having a kind of innocence. The talk had changed to the Gaelic, which none of the players could understand, but oddly they could make themselves clear in French.

Arrived at Cawdor, one more grim castle with tales of a kidnapped heiress, Will seized the chance to evade the bustle of arrival and took himself up to the moor. As so often he needed time and space to think, and here it was solitary enough. The light was long at the time of year and he could see, in the near distance among the waters of the firth, the Black Isle rearing. A north-easter hit him coldly as he walked, then sat on a great stone to take his bearings. The ling heather was over and the bell was out, flowering purple as far as the eye could see, with small hunched cranberries clustered sharp red among them. By night it would be an eerie place, fit for witches.

The priest and he had talked on the way back from Glamis, and Father Huntly, on hearing Will's interest in the old long-dead king, had said he could use such images to help the English Catholics, who suffered much and lacked direct instruction. "The figure of the old king could mean the Church," he said. "Your phrase, *Who would have thought the old man had so much blood in him?* is apt; who would have thought that, with the tortures and the martyrdoms, the Church would survive in England at all, over sixty years? It is as long since Henry VIII destroyed the monks' hospice of Lewes Priory, which cured and helped many folk since the Conquest. That was the beginning of't, and next went Becket's tomb at Canterbury, a shrine for centuries. The king and Cromwell gave the Carthusians dogs' lives before the traitors' death for eight of them, while many hung in chains from the prison walls. Elizabeth has made more martyrs than ever her half-sister Mary, for all they bay about Foxe's book and the burning of Latimer, who mocked a slow-burning priest himself from the pulpit in his heyday."

"There is less of that here in Scotland, with the king's toleration."

"That will not endure if contention ever arises between papal supremacy and the king's. The Kirk has induced prudence rather than fear in some; in the north at Cardell, an Ogilvie destroyed all evidence of the birth of his heir by a Catholic wife, and sent the boy abroad, hoping to lose him. The son of the second wife prospers, and will inherit; but John Ogilvie has found his way to us, and his wit and courage will stand him in good stead when, as he asks, he is sent back here to Scotland when I myself am old and, maybe, occupied abroad wi' affairs o' the Order."

"What do you want me to do?" asked Will. "I have a wife and children, and dare not risk prison or worse, even if only for their sakes. I am no hero, father."

"Put in a message here and there among your lines that Catholic listeners will understand, if only to keep their hearts high. You know what you will write, and how to express it."

It was then, mentioning the play he thought of about Macbeth, that the priest had told him, idly, a tale still remembered at Cawdor; a wise woman had met the mormaer, as he had been then, on a moor here, and had told him he would be thane twice and the third time, king of the land. "It was not yet called Scotland. Its name was Albán. Later, Malcolm Céann Mór, who killed Macbeth to avenge Duncan his father, was called the best king who ever reigned in Albán. Moreover Duncan had the better right, being the son of Bethoc, dochter to Malcolm II who died at Glamis. She had mairrit Crinan the Thane. Macbeth had royal blood, but was sideways related. He mairrit a princess of the old line. Her name was Gruoch. It is not a name found any more."

Gruoch, Lady Macbeth, washing her hands to free them of the blood of gracious Duncan, the old king, the Church. Anne Boleyn, crazed with remorse in the Tower.

On the moor, in the darkening light, he saw not one wise woman but three; his three witches, culled from the memory of galloping Bothwell and the vision after. Three hags on a moor, chanting spells over a cauldron. Barbara Napier, Annis Sampson, and the third was his dark lady. *Hail to thee, Macbeth, that shalt be king hereafter*.

He could, if the play were ever presented before the real king, maybe by then in England, have a dinner with a mirror held, showing all the kings of Scotland from Malcolm Céann Mór, including old King Blearie and his twenty-two bairns. They could be in the imagination of the beholder, the murderer. By then, nemesis would be approaching, but it would praise the Stuarts.

It was comfortless meantime, here on a stone on a bleak moor. He began to long for Christmas, home, Stratford, and the sight of his son Hamnet again. He would be walking by now, with frequent falls, picked up by his mother or, perhaps, Susanna. So much time had passed that they would have grown out of recognition. He had no complaints about having come on this journey, however. They had been made welcome here in the north parts, feasted and showered with praise and money. He had tasted their venison and their whisky, and had heard their varying tongues. He had a wealth of ideas to take home. He hoped the plague had subsided in London. He wondered how old Pembroke and young Southampton, both patrons, fared. W.H., only sixteen, and he were planning a new theatre together. He must introduce the Catholic messages sparingly, but it added the spice of danger as well as serving God.

God had better servants. He thought of Campion, tortured beyond feeling before his appalling death; Cecil had said, when the future priest left earlier to train abroad, that England had lost one of her diamonds. Then there was the saying carved in the stones of the Tower of London by a man who had been kept confined now nine years, not permitted to know when his wife bore him a son. The queen had sent word that it was a daughter, hoping to beguile him into denying his faith in exchange for freedom. *Quanto afflictionis pro Christo in hoc saeculo tanto plus gloriae cum Christo in futuro.*

They said the earl of Arundel was sick and near death now, but he had awaited it daily for many years since the axe's edge had been turned against him at his trial. He, William Shakespeare, had endured no such testing. God must have allotted him some other destiny. He would never jettison the world's rewards, and knew it.

He rose and left the moor, and went back to the others. He was greeted by an invitation to go and read to Sir Walter Ogilvie and his lady at Drum. The players were to travel on to Elgin. "I will await ye at the inn in Keith, and we can ride on to Elgin together," the priest had said. He would evidently not visit the father of young John Ogilvie, and his second wife. He vouchsafed the information that she had been one of the Seven Pearls of Lochleven.

Later on return to Keith, Will related that it was old Lady Mar, the terrifying dowager met with at Blair, who had caused Sir Walter Ogilvie to invite him to Drum. The king's Lady Minny was a kinswoman by marriage, her husband having been an Erskine; and the Pearl of Lochleven, grown solid now with loss of youth and childbearing, maintained the dark stern looks of her grandmother, somehow seduced into bearing James V the late Regent Moray. Her one unmarred sister Jean had been among those listening to his recital of *Venus and Adonis*, and had the same features and expression, that of somebody who can never be wrong. There had been several young folk, including James the usurping heir, also a daughter of Sir Walter by his first marriage, a suppressed creature who had been suitably married, while still young, to Sir John Forbes of Pitsligo. She would be a full sister of the missing John, but doubtless knew nothing of him.

"There was an awkwardness amang the Pearls when ane o' them, Elizabeth, mairrit the earl o' Erroll against the king's will," said Father Huntly. "Erroll is a stiff papist, as they ca' it, and has been in trouble more than ance for communing wi' Spain and refusing to conform to the Kirk's religion. He and my brother the earl may cause trouble together yet."

He looked at Will suddenly, perhaps with appeal. "There is another reason why I would not visit Drum," he said. "The Ogilvies and the Gordons ha'e a feud o' our ain, as strong as that wi' Moray earlier. It stems from the ungoverned fleshly passion of our kinswoman Bessie Gordon o' Caithness, a dean's dochter. She had overmuch love for my brother John."

His mouth set into repressive lines, and Will knew an instant's sympathy with Bessie. Love would out, despite everything. Of all the nine brothers, only this one seemed to have denied the demands of the body and followed his Jesuit calling. It made him harsh with those who were weak in such respects.

"It was a devious business," he said. "Bessie got old Sandy Ogilvie, laird o' estates, to marry her, and persuaded him to disown his heir James, naming instead my ain brother John Gordon. It was done, and James Ogilvy of Cardell – they spell the name as they will – lost his inheritance while my brother John gained it. That was in the time when they hangit the cardinal. I mysel' was in Paris."

"It was perhaps better to be there than here in those days," murmured Will. He was touched by the way Father Huntly had come out of his self-imposed shell by degrees, and by now would talk to him as he must talk to few. The closed and dedicated circle of his brothers in Christ maybe discouraged converse except about their vocation.

"Sune auld Ogilvie died, worn out wi' matrimony, and Bessie mairrit my brother John at once, hardly waiting for the burial." *The funeral baked meats did coldly furnish forth the marriage tables*. "They enjoyed the lands and rents thegither until the Queen Regent, who had enough ither troubles on her hands, took Cardell's part, as did her dochter

Queen Mary when she cam' hame frae France. Between them the twa queens put matters richt as far as it micht then be done, compensating my brother John wi' lesser lands, but the ill-feeling remains. I fear my clan, the Huntlys, do not come well out of that affair and others."

"I can see the towers of Elgin," said Will.

The ruins of the great cathedral reared out of what was still bright day. The air was balmy and cool, here among what had once been the Lantern of the North. Edward I of England had destroyed it in the last phase of his vicious march three centuries ago, which had begun by burning Berwick. He had failed to bring the Scots to heel. Will had begun to understand, as far as an Englishman born could do, the loathing of the name still, in Scotland. He had seen the charred remains of what had been David I's great jewelled chain of abbeys across the Border, burned in Henry VIII's Rough Wooing of the child Queen Mary for his late-got son. The Lamp of Lothian was darkened in Haddington, Perth ruined, a new way of thinking imposed and paid for with English money. He and his players had been made welcome less as Englishmen than as Kate, Petruchio, Grumio and Bianca. That was his mission, to heal feuds; also, to bring in secret reminders, as the priest had suggested, as and when he could. Those must be thought out carefully, ready to be denied wide-eyed.

Meantime they would meet and rehearse in Elgin itself. There were houses nearby to which they might be asked. Then there would be Strathbogie, then last of all Dunrobin in Sutherland, where the priest would leave them following a reunion, after long, with his sister Jean.

Jean had for a time been the wife of Queen Mary's Bothwell. It was impossible to escape, anywhere in her realm, from some reminder of the luckless queen, the king's magical and unforgotten mother.

At Dunrobin, he would ask about the handkerchief.

They came north-east to Gordon country at last, and the sight of Huntly's fine new mansion of Strathbogie. Hitherto the great houses in which the troupe had played, or in which Shakespeare had read, still bore their ancestral character of having been erected long ago as fortresses; even Aldie had been described lately as "a castle of marvellous strength". Only at Blair had there been signs of change, of making houses comfortable to live in as was being done in England over the last reigns.

Huntly, evidently trusting in his own power in the north, and standing with the king, had gone even further. Will had never seen for himself the grand châteaux of the Loire which in their turn had been inspired by the French invasions of Italy last century. He had heard from others of the delicate marvels, mansard roofs, moulded ceilings, planned formal gardens. No doubt Huntly's upbringing in France, and his half-French wife and mother-in-law, had influenced him also. What must initially have been a plain stone tower of refuge and strength, built at the time of Bannockburn, had been transformed.

There were not even the saffron-shirted torch-tenders at the door, for lighted sconces would have blackened the new walls. Everywhere reared tall wax candles in silver sconces with long-handled dousers attached. Not a Highlander was in sight except for those who later bore in the trestles and the meat, also a piper who walked round and round, playing airs which, as Will already knew, made talk difficult to hear. It was said the pipes were best heard across a mountain range, but the piper himself was a fine sight with his plaid over his shoulder, his dagger in his stocking, and his dark kilt swinging as they had swung at Cleator Moor. Will kept to himself his knowledge of that early history, during the wars between Stephen and Matilda. Matilda's uncle, David I of Scotland and the chain of abbeys, had become a warrior for her sake and her dead mother's, his sister, and had brought what the English thought were dancing-girls until they saw them fight.

The chief dined himself, at his high table, with few guests. Shakespeare met him after dinner. Huntly had a hangdog look, with less assurance than could have been expected given his reputation as young Moray's murderer. His manner was a mixture of ruffian and *grand seigneur*. He fondled his pretty countess's upper arms possessively. She was again expecting a child, and there were more in the nursery. Will decided to speak with her about the strawberry handkerchief as soon as it might be done. However meantime, with dinner over, he ran about in his capacity of stage-manager, making ready for the plays. There were to be two tonight and one tomorrow, then he and the priest must ride. Huntly himself, he heard, had been attainted by the Kirk's council in Fife. No doubt that accounted for his dolorous expression, though Fife was a long way off.

The play sufficed; even Huntly's French mother-in-law laughed in her weeds. Patrick Gordon, the second brother, guffawed loudly, sparking off the rest. Soon the hall rocked with laughter, drowning out many of the actors' lines, but by then nobody cared. Shakespeare himself saw the fine new hall in a haze of blurred candlelight, the faces merging into another, featureless; he had been plied with French wine. The piper struck up a wail again, then a harper came in to play; that was a relief. Huntly beckoned Will over, and talked in a low voice throughout the Gaelic songs. It was as though he felt the constant need to explain himself, in a sickly and pious fashion that ill became him. Shakespeare tried not to remember the mangled, greening face of the

Bonnie Earl on the king's closet wall, back in Holyrood. The earl nonetheless spoke of it.

"Ye will ha'e heard o' me, nae doubt, as a man o' bluid. I ken fine all men blame me for the Moray murder. They tak' sma' account o' the feud that has been between our clans for lang." His finger pointed to his wine-cup, which a Highlander came and refilled. "Folk blame me for overmuch. I am blamed for the regent Lennox's deith, but that was Lord Claud Hamilton, Paisley by this as ye ken. He has reaped a reward he didna fairly gain."

The earl took a swig at his wine-cup. His speech had not the intonation used here, any more than his wife's. Henrietta Huntly spoke little, however, except to talk in French with her mother and her younger sister, married to Mar and in a like state to herself. Will gathered that her husband was to come and fetch her home. He doubted if it was an easy situation for one of Esmé Stuart's daughters to be married to the papist Huntly and the other to the opposing Mar.

Maybe they had agreed to settle their differences. Meantime, Huntly himself sat and twirled his wine-cup by the stem, admiring its silver chasing. "Ken ye the Italian tongue, Maister Shakespeare?" Will knew he was being tested; presently he would be asked if he knew Spanish.

He smiled, cat-like, above his small narrow beard.

"Some little, my lord, culled from Dante by way of mild acquaintance. I can by no means rival you in French." He had long learned to flatter patrons. Patrick Gordon, who had been listening, broke in roughly.

"Why did ye talk o' the murder o' Lennox the king's grandsire? These English will think we do naught but kill."

"Having glimpsed fair Strathbogie, I know otherwise. There is nothing like it in England, save perhaps the queen's Nonsuch."

That pleased the earl. Huntly went on to talk of how the

house was so newly completed that builders' rubble still lay about the back, where he planned French gardens in the manner of the Valois palaces. "My wife and her mither are weel acquaint wi' gardens o' the kind. They will maybe show ye the morn what we ha'e begun."

Will knew he had made his opportunity. Next day, he joined the countess, her sister and her mother in the new gardens, where the beginnings of knot-patterns had already been planted. There was other company; Henrietta's brother, the duke of Lennox, who had been present in silence at dinner, had joined them; and young George, Lord Enzie and Gordon, a handsome child who clung to his grandmother's skirts. Esmé Stuart's widow was the most forceful character present, though she said little. It could be imagined that she had ordered her elegant husband, so greatly loved by the king. She wore her rustling weeds like armour, the crucifix on her breast gleaming openly. If my lords of the Kirk met with her, they would lose the argument.

Walking among the newmade paths, Will sought out Countess Henrietta. "My lady, I would have a quiet word; can that be done? It concerns the king." James, he knew, had always been kind to her, regarding her as a daughter. Her clear eyes surveyed him; there were things that could not be said here.

"My mother has brought me a Holland hawk," she said. "Come with me and Ludovic, and we will ride to Gight together. You will like to see the nesting herons." She had pronounced Gight correctly as Geicht. She seemed to have forgotten her state; was it advisable to ride? He asked outright, French women were less prudish than his own on such matters. Henrietta smiled.

"There is George here already, and two brothers. In any case we will travel gently. Ludo will come; we are safe with him. There will be leisure to talk."

That it would delay his own journey did not matter, but he knew himself to be no fine horseman such as should ride in the train of a noble lady. He was used to workaday cobs, no more. As regarded hawking, he had once owned a haggard in Stratford days, but had returned her to her woods when he left for London. In the quick way she had of reading his thoughts the countess said, "It will be but tame sport. My lord has taken the great peregrine to himself, and left me the tercel."

They rode out into a fine day, the Holland hawk on Henrietta's wrist. Ludovic Lennox rode alongside, still in silence. He was a sad man, having lost his young wife scarcely two years before; she had been, as Will ascertained, a Ruthven, one of Gowrie's daughters. Henrietta Huntly, when they rode forward alone, told Will he had no desire to marry the Campbell widow the king had thought of for him, but one must not offend the king.

This allowed Will to put his question. Quickly and in a low voice, he told her the story of the strawberry handkerchief, had she received it, and would she, if so, return it to the king? "He has few things of his mother's," he added persuasively.

Henrietta let fly the Holland hawk. It was to bring back a field-mouse, a squealing stoat, and finally a mallard at the Wells of Ythan. "It is not to be a good day," she said, and lowered her long eyelashes. She had a toughness that would make her a survivor, her sister lacked it, and was woebegone at the thought of parting with their mother and returning with Mar. That last had not yet appeared when they left, and Marie his lady had not ridden out with them. This expected occasion of hers was to be one of thirteen. Henrietta herself would bear nine children to the earl. She accepted her lot, evidently.

"I would always oblige the king, but the queen does not

like me, as Huntly killed her lover. I would be the last one she would tell."

She loosened rein, and rode on; evidently she would say nothing more. He followed, with the silent Lennox. Will had an echo of a line come to him, not his own but from some ballad:

O, they rade on, and further on,
And rade in red blude to the knee,
For a' the blude that's shed on earth
Runs through the streams o' that countrie.

There seemed no reason for remembering it, here in this comely company.

They came to a deep chasm where the river ran loudly beneath. "In the winter it carries snow," said Henrietta. "Over there, between the trees, you may see the castle of my lord's kin. We will not go in, as you have your journey soon." She smiled. "They are a wild clan, forever feuding. The first laird fell at Flodden. Look at the herons nesting in their trees." She pointed with her whip to where the great grey birds flapped or else rested; he saw one return with a fish in its beak, still writhing. "Thomas the Rhymer wrote a prophecy about Gight," the countess said. "He could foretell such things. He saw the death of good King Alexander four days before it chanced that the king fell over a cliff. After that there were the wars with you English." She was mocking him.

"What are the lines he wrote about Gight?" he asked, ignoring the taunt. He listened to her low and pleasant voice, hearing, beyond it, another, not the sound of the river.

"*When the heron leaves the tree, The laird o' Gight will landless be*," recited Henrietta. "At some time in the future, the timber will be sold off and the trees cut down, and all the herons will leave." She sounded as if it would certainly happen. Will saw the narrow castle, just perceived between the trees. There was still a voice, strong and certain as his own, coming on the wind. He remembered the clarsach player in Edinburgh, with his song by James V.

We'll go no more a-roving
So late into the night.

It was different, no longer in the dead king's braid Scots. This was out of the future. So was the play he was still to write, with a character in it named Berowne, Biron . . .

"You are hearing some strange thing," said Henrietta. "You are not like the rest, a hired player. It is as though you had the Sight they have here, and yet you are an Englishman."

He did not answer.

"Let us ride back," said Henrietta. "My lord does not like me long out of his sight, although he knows I used to hunt with the best of them, beside the king at Falkland and in the Woods of Keir. The king rides swiftly; he is no longer ill at ease in the saddle."

The killed mallard hung limply across hers. Will knew he had got no further about the missing handkerchief. He must think now of putting on *The Shrew* for a farewell to Strathbogie.

On their return, the earl of Mar had arrived, and would wait, not too willingly, with his wife to see the play. He had the stern Erskine darkness, and their self-righteous air; but he had been a friend and companion to young James VI in their schooldays, and the king, beaten by him at some task or other, always called him Slaitis. Yet another, present quietly among the women at last night's dinner, sat watching *The Shrew*, by now a finished performance. She was Patrick Gordon's wife, having formerly been married to one of the wild Gordons of Gight. Before that, she had been the daughter of the hanged Cardinal Betoun and his faithful mistress Marion Ogilvy. All that would be one more story he, William Shakespeare, dared not write. The Cardinal had sat, triumphant in his robes, to watch the burning of young George Wishart, a schoolmaster who had taught the New Testament in Greek and had preached the beliefs of Luther. Swift revenge came when the reformers hanged the cardinal out of his own castle window at St. Andrews, piddling into his opened mouth. Kit Marlowe would have made a play of it, maybe, as he cared for none. He, Will, as always, had to be careful. There was in any case no message for suppressed English Catholics in the story, except maybe to point out the brief nature of earthly power.

Riding away, seeing the last of fair Strathbogie, he took time to wonder about Queen Anna's dislike of the young countess, if it existed. Henrietta had implied that the Bonnie Earl had been the queen's lover, whereas as far as anyone knew, he had merely partnered her in the dance. Maybe belief in the matter had grown with hearing the song so often sung in taverns. He had not been asked to play before the earl's old mother at Doune.

He had in any case added certain lines to Kate's speech about the duty owed to husbands, while Huntly leered at his returned wife. "I would not have thrown down a new hat," had said the young countess afterwards. The brief accord they had felt on the ride had gone, as was expedient. Regarding the strawberry handkerchief, it was certain she knew more than she had said. He had done as much as he might in the matter.

Having ridden some way, he turned his head to look back

at the fair house. It was as if he foresaw its doom. Within a year, and by the king's own order, Strathbogie would be burned to ashes.

"My sister Jean will make ye forget a' other places ye ha'e seen," said the priest as they rode into Sutherland. "I ha'e always loved her the best o' us a'."

Will was silent, noting how greatly more human Father Huntly had become during the times they had spent together. It seemed in another life that he had first seen him in the cellar in the Canongate house. As for Lady Jean Sutherland, whom he was about to meet, he had heard of her; everyone in both countries had. As Lady Jean Gordon she had been married briefly to the late Bothwell, and had divorced him for adultery with a maidservant in order that he might marry Queen Mary. It seemed an unsavoury tale.

"When ye say naught, and ask no questions, I ken it is because the matter is in your heid a'ready," said the priest perspicaciously. "I doubt it will be in the way the world thinks, however, which is not the whole truth."

"If you will honour me with the whole truth, I will keep silence."

"As ye will; Bothwell now is deid, and can neither suffer mair hairm nor inflict it. My sister is like mysel', and Huntly despite everything, a Catholic. Yet she was suffered to make a Kirk marriage wi' a man already mairrit and about to marry again. Like the sixth earl o' Angus, the earl o' Bothwell handfasted his way through life. When he mairrit Jean he'd already promised marriage to the woman in Norway who betrayed him at last, also to another in France; and afore that to a widow on the Border, who'd been wife to a Scott o' Buccleuch. It was not that he was what they ca' a ladies' man, he was over rough for that; but he couldna see ayont the present. He was, as they say, a fule for himsel'; and, God knows, he paid."

"I hope your sister is happy now, with a new husband and children." It was all he could think of to say. Had the lovesome queen of Scots been no more than one step higher on the ladder of ambition? Had she never touched Bothwell's heart? Nobody now could say. There had been a rumour spread, out of spite against the queen, that after his marriage to her Bothwell had returned to Lady Jean and kept her as his mistress. All else apart, with the events that had crowded in, there would not have been leisure. It was doubtless a lie spread by the queen's enemies, to lessen tales of her charm.

"She didna marry, Jean, till a'maist the year o' Bothwell's deith in Denmark, twenty year ago that would be. She maybe wouldna ha'e done so even then, but for pity. Sutherland had been poisoned in youth, and never yet enjoys health; and they'd forced him to marry an older bride who was unsuitable. Jean saved his soul. He loves her, relies on her like a bairn, and their children are bonnie. She prays daily, I ken, for his soul and Bothwell's, and that of the late queen."

They had come at last within sight of Dunrobin, its high round turret rearing on a sharply defined rock set among green hills. It proved, however, to be like entering a small country town. Shakespeare had never seen hillsides as busy; they were scattered with bothans, in which the clan families lived. Being a fine day – the weather on the whole had been kind on this venture, the only heavy rain having been in the west, after leaving Paisley – being so, everyone seemed to be outside, even the old folk sitting at their doors telling their beads, a thing seldom seen now openly elsewhere in Scotland, or anywhere in Britain. "My sister encourages them in it; her own are never out of her hand save when she

f

hath some other occupation," remarked Father James. "She takes the children in their catechism, for it is seldom that I, or any other priest, find leisure to come; and when we do we are made greatly welcome. There will be mass in the open, please God, for everyone tomorrow."

Will, riding past, had a view of everyone at whatever they chose to be at; digging, hoeing, gleaning in the small rigged fields, piling up stocks of oat-straw, with one particular old woman nearby in a hood, who looked up and smiled and bobbed, then went back to her grinding of threshed oats to make meal for porridge. She was turning a great round stone with a handle with another beneath, so that the oats were crushed between the two and the fine meal spurted into a long trough. As soon as it was full it was emptied into bowls brought by the other women, all of whom had brought their oats for grinding. The work was heavy, and he saw the next woman waiting to take her turn at the stones. It was a scene such as might have been witnessed from very old time. A short distance off, kilted men in saffron shirts, such as he had seen worn in the Canongate, went by in a short careful procession carrying four or five beehives. "They are bringing the bees back frae the heather," Father James told him. "Jean culls the hives hersel', and never lets them swarm."

A young girl, perhaps eleven years old, passed by in the near distance as they rode; she was leading a flock of goats to vary their pasture, her long skirts kilted up for easy walking. She waved cheerfully. "That is my niece Mary," said the priest, nodding to her. "She has grown sin' I saw her last; that will be three year syne. She is a wheen spoilt, being ane lass amang mony brithers, and her father's favourite. Her only sister is mairrit and away. Mary hersel' was contracted suitably eneuch as an infant, but says she will wait to choose her ain husband. There is time yet, to be sure." His face brightened. "There, at the door now, is my sister Jean."

He did not sound emotional, for it was not his dry way; but when a great lady, modestly clad in a kirtle and round hood framing her prudent face, and dangling at her belt the largest pair of dark beads Will had ever seen, hurried out to greet them, the brother and sister embraced with joy, and clung for moments together.

"Jamie! After sae lang, and ye are safe! How fares Willie in Paris?" That was yet another of the Gordon brotherhood, who had elected to live on in France.

"Weel eneuch," replied the priest briefly. "Ah, Jean, ye ha'e changed but little."

It was not, Shakespeare thought, a face which time would ravage, having fine bones. Her eyes were clear, full and bright as a young leveret's he had once come upon in a Warwickshire field. They were the eyes that had once gazed into Bothwell's as his wedded wife. He found himself unable to picture the queen as more desirable. This was a woman in a thousand.

"We all change," she said quietly. "Who is this wayfarer?" Shakespeare saw himself as he must appear to her, balding now he had removed his cap, travel-stained, unknown.

Father James explained everything, and Will added that the troupe would follow and he hoped would please her. "It will divert my lord to see a play," replied the Countess of Sutherland. Her brother asked then how the earl fared. His wife shook her head sadly.

"Ever the worse, I fear." She turned to Will. "My husband has never been in full health since his youth, when a kinswoman at Golspie poisoned him and his father and stepmother at supper, hoping for the title for her ain son." She preceded them inside the castle, speaking still, "She made this error, however; she poisoned the son as weel. My husband lived on, saved maybe by his youth; but he has never since been richt, and his parents the earl and countess were carried back here to Dunrobin to die. I mysel' met my lord later on, for my brither Thomas Gordon had mairrit wi' his sister Jean."

Shakespeare was aware that he had been informed of the existence of yet one more of the Huntly brothers. The countess sent for wine, and Father James told him in a low voice that being young the unfortunate earl, still weak from poison, had been put in charge of a greedy and unscrupulous guardian, who had forced Sutherland to marry a much older kinswoman of his own. "She was a wanton," said the countess roundly. "My lord rid himsel' o' her later by law, saying he had been forced to it, and mairrit mysel'." Her lips closed on the rest and she looked down at her hands, which bore a single wedding ring. One felt nevertheless that the memory of Bothwell remained with her through all her busy and useful life. He would not have asked concerning that time; she lived for the day and the hour, as Christ had ordained.

The castle was snugly furnished, a comfortable home. Afterwards, sharing their wine, he found her smiling at him. "How was that for a tale of poisonings? Do not, I pray, put us on the boards as we are; but all ye see and hear will be like meat and drink, I don't doubt."

"I will not, my lady." Nevertheless the image of many corpses, dead of poison and carried off stage, had come. Father and stepmother, mother and stepfather, a seducer? There must be a watcher uncertain of himself, and flawed; a philosopher who thought before he acted. Death must be the result of all of it, at the end, after much ruminating aloud. Audiences liked a death. He wondered when he would meet the earl, no doubt an invalid. Jean Gordon had had compassion on him, and now was a woman content. Had the vainglorious Bothwell – the term was not his own – regretted parting with her, already scarred with his Border feuds as he had been? Will already knew the tale was whispered still in England that after giving him up by divorce and the marriage to Mary Stuart, Bothwell's former wife had remained his mistress. Seeing her now he did not believe it. The tale had been put about by the queen's enemies, denying her the power to charm men. Mary Stuart had since charmed many to their deaths; but this woman would be no man's whore.

She beckoned now to a servant who did not wear the tartan or saffron, but a tunic brightly patterned with crosses and crowns. She addressed him as Gomez, and bade him tell them to prepare food for all who came. "He is Spanish, and my steward," she explained to Will. "He is one of the Armada sailors who did not drown. Instead, some were washed up on the north shore, others on the islands. The folk there are learning to knit in the way the Spaniards teach them. It is a peaceful end to what micht ha'e been war, of which we, in Scotland, are still suspected."

The wine had been excellent, home-brewed from last summer's elderflowers. Will had seldom tasted better in all his journeyings: and King Philip's man had served it. He had heard of sailors knitting to pass the long spells at sea, but had never before seen this rich patterning. The tale would interest his friend Southampton, who liked such things about him. The priest said little, drinking his wine but fixing his eyes on Jean, as though the sight of her refreshed him more.

"I would dearly love to tell my wife how to make this wine," Will said. The elderflowers would be over in Stratford now till next year, but it would be pleasant, after that, to drink it with the children running about the room. The thought brought them nearer.

"There maun ha'e been nae rain when ye pick them. Wait for a dry week, then pick each flo'er frae the stalk, else that makes the taste bitter if it's left. Then make the wine like ony ither. Your wife will ken weel eneuch."

"She comes of farming folk." He wanted her to know it. Jean filled his stoup again; he noted that at times she used the Lowland Scots he had grown used to hear, then at others a speech without accent. It was not the Gaelic they had up here, but a pure sound like English itself. Will stopped her halfway.

"My lady, I will be drunk, and when I am drunk I give vein too greatly to my tongue. Tell me of your many brothers. I have met Sir Patrick and the earl, and their wives."

Well, there had been Thomas, who married poor Jean, but Jean was dead the other year; and Robert, who had been killed by a gun. Alexander the first-born had died young; she did not remember him. Adam, the famous Edom o' Gordon, he had heard of already regarding the Towie burnings. "The queen's Marie Fleming, who mairrit Maitland o' Lethington, put in a word for him, and he was warded in a town and told not to leave it, but no town would contain Adam. There is Willie also in Paris, and the two ye ha'e met. Then there is John; we do not speak of John." That would be Bessie Ogilvie's lover, who had caused the feud. "The Forbeses and my clan fell out also, and one followed Adam abroad to kill him, but he didna contrive it. It is by far more peacefu' here than in the south parts, Maister Shakespeare."

The trundling sound of the cart from Elgin had come, beyond in the yard. Jean Sutherland rose and went to find Gomez, returning shortly. "There is venison for their supper, and after that the play if he will, and then my bothan folk will gi'e them gude rest. Dry heather stems covered over wi' bracken make a finer bed than down."

There was no sign yet of the invalid earl, as the priest was with him. Later Father James came out to where they were and said my lord of Sutherland would greatly like to watch the play. "It diverts him to think I might be in it, but we will leave that here, I think." He had acted several parts on the way, all of them convincingly. It was the fate of many of his Order to disguise themselves as horse-copers, pedlars, even harpers if they could sing.

He looked now about the hall; the countess had gone to her husband. He told Will then in a low voice that the Sutherlands had once almost provided a king for Scotland by way of a younger daughter of Robert the Bruce. "That one was a full sister o' King Davie, for there were several born to the king and queen, his parents, after her release frae English prison. The young man died, however, o' the plague while held hostage in London, and so we have the Stewart line frae puir Marjory, deid afore King David was born. Her son and the king didna deal weel thegither, but in the end King Blearie, first of the Stewarts, was crowned at Scone. He had been a valiant fighter, and earned his croun. After that the succession was agreed, except that his sons fell out in turn. One o' them starved his brither's heir to deith, leaving a young prince o' twelve. Since Robert III every king has come to his throne a child. Woe to the land, Scripture says."

"Times are perhaps better now." Will was hardly listening to the tragedy of the royal house. A letter had been brought by the troupe from Elgin. It was from W.H., Southampton the younger, assuring him that plague in the capital had subsided and that the theatres would open again soon. Everyone craved his return, and he himself was eager now to go, the priest having been conveyed to his destination. He himself would make greater haste on his way back, stopping at fewer houses. As it turned out, there was to be one more stopping-place for him in Edinburgh, besides again seeing the king. Not to do so would be seen as a slight, a mistake, no doubt, for the future. However he had failed James completely over the matter of the strawberry handkerchief.

The play went well, the earl smiled languidly from his cushioned long-settle, and his countess sat beside him with her hands folded for once, and her young daughter at her feet. Sutherland himself had the face of an old man from the long weakness draining his body. He was returned to his bedchamber while the rest of them had music from small pipes, and the players cleared the hall. Will decided that from the look of him the earl would soon die; and wondered who, for there would assuredly be some, would offer for so useful and loving a wife. She reminded him of the woman in scripture; *thyself shall eat what thou hast toiled to win . . . fruitful as the vine in the heart of thy home, the children round thy table sturdy as olive branches*. Two of her boys were at school in Dornoch; the wayward Mary had had her skirts made seemly again and her hair smoothed. Countess Jean was telling her beads again absently, as though she did this of her own accord when there was no other occupation. Will again wondered if she prayed for the soul of Bothwell among the rest. Chained like a beast in prison till he died in Denmark, she might well do so; but a woman openly praying with beads would never now be seen in England, or in the south of this country.

Denmark, the bleak place from which the queen had come. It would perhaps make a fitting scene for a play, almost as much so as Scotland. Shakespeare wanted to get back to pens and paper, what he had with him was long used up with notes taken on the way.

However Will savoured the lingering smell of venison,

roasted and gleaming with basted fat as it had been, so that they had all eaten their fill of that and the oaten bread made here. Jean Sutherland had seen to it that the best cut went first to my lord, carried in on a silver dish. The earl was a fortunate man; the last part of his life had surely atoned for its early sorrows.

Next day, having spent a pleasant night in a bed with fresh linen – no heather stems and dry bracken for him – Will was shown the dairy, where round pale cheeses from young Mary's goats were maturing, like the wine in great jars in the cellar, and the honeycombs in the buttery. He was not offered any food, for no one had eaten yet; there was to be mass held in the open. Everyone from the castle and the bothans would be present, both old and young. They came down from the hillsides quietly, kneeling on the grass; it was like the feeding of the five thousand. Father James, two young boys following, emerged vested into the early sunlight, the carried candles flickering pale against the day. Will, kneeling with the rest, saw Spanish Gomez make ready to help serve, wearing laundered linen over his tunic. This was as it must have been in old times in early England, with whole villages worshipping together as one, each aiding each, the old on the arm of the younger, the children led without fear. It seemed impossible that these round green hills should ever be bare of folk, like those of Northumbria; yet Northumbria, in St. Cuthbert's day, would have witnessed such masses, with kings in their crowns present to serve. Surely no English conqueror would ever come to destroy the life here in Sutherland, as had been done among the Border hills, making them a desert. Will thought of such a fantasy, even while Father James raised the Host; shortly he watched the passing by of these douce, productive folk, clad in their best, the men with knives sheathed, the women with their heads covered in the comely arisaid, carrying their children for a blessing, the older ones close to their skirts. The greed of an English king had destroyed all this in the south. Jean herself took these folk by custom for instruction, priests being scarce. A mass itself was rare enough. He received the broken bread at last on his tongue and saw Gomez drain the wine.

After breakfast Father James said his farewells. "I am grateful for your protection," he told Will. "I doubt not ye will make some noise in the world. It has been pleasant to have your company. I have learned much from you, and doubtless you some small thing from me."

He smiled, and both knew what he meant. He added that he intended taking ship from the firth after visiting his nephews at Dornoch school. "Then, if God wills, I will return to Paris for a time. There will be much business waiting."

From a Jesuit, formidable scholars as they were known to be, it was a compliment to be told his own company had not been tedious. Will himself regretted the priest's going; he had enjoyed the stimulation to his own mind, and his spirit was refreshed by the masses. He did not witness the parting between brother and sister, but when he met with Jean again her eyes were tear-filled.

"Ye wadna think o' him as the finest Hebrew scholar in three kingdoms," she said, "going about amang the puir folk the way he does. It may well be another three years afore he is returned, and there is aye the risk of prison."

"The king turns a blind eye."

"Maybe. However there may well come a time, for my brother the priest fashes certain anes on the council wi' his comings and goings, and his conversions to the auld faih in Scotland, that they procure a sentence o' banishment upon

Father James Gordon. It is because the king has an affection for my eldest brother the earl o' Huntly, or at any rate owes him favours, that my brother the priest has been left to honour his vocation. As ye say, never tell me the king kens naught o't. There is little the sixth James Stuart fails to jalouse and ken."

Shakespeare was left thinking how the English language lacked any word such as jalouse, when she turned her clear eyes on him. They were filled with sudden appeal.

"When ye win back to England, maister, will it be wi' the memory o' a woman who deserted a forsaken man? Had Bothwell had need o' me, I'd stayed alane; but by the end, with him a prisoner tied to a stake, and his mind gane, what gude could I da'e him except by prayer? That he has aye had, and has still. How could I deprive my present lord, who was sick and needed me? Not all things are talked of in the auld queen's councils in London. A' they ken o' me is that I was Bothwell's wife and am no longer, and that he is deid these ten year." She turned away. "Queen Mary is so now, near seeven. I kenned her, naebody could help but love her; how could I act other than I did when she was found to be in the state she was after Dunbar, when Bothwell ravished her?"

"I do not know." That had been a dangerous time. They had said the whole thing was planned from the beginning, that the Lady Jean Gordon of Huntly, a papist, should be content with a Protestant ceremony that could presently be set aside. Her brothers would know, if she did not, of Bothwell's earlier handfastings.

"I wish with a' my heart," said Jean Sutherland now, "that the twin boys he got on the queen had lived. What she endured at Lochleven caused her to miscarry. Like my ain brother James, they would ha'e caused a deal o' fash."

The bright hare's eyes were sparkling, then she grew

grave again, fingering her great dark beads. "These are my comfort," she said. "I will pray for Bothwell and the queen till my ain deith. Wherever their souls are, they will maybe ken o' my prayers."

"You could have done no other," Shakespeare said. "It was fate, such as used to overtake the Greeks."

"Weel, they say we are maisters o' our fate. That is as it should be. I acted as I felt to be richt."

"Pray for me also, if you will," he said. "Your brother has given me a task. I will carry it out as best I can. Think of the good you do here, the cheer you have brought the earl, who was once a sad man." He smiled. "You know, my lady, what was said and written; *you have kept the best wine till now*. I will not soon forget your elderflower wine."

She was silent for moments, then rose. "The priest my brother left some matter to be given ye when he had gane," she said. "I ha'e it in my kist in the tower, come up."

They ascended worn twisting steps together, coming at last to a tower room Jean kept for her private use. A small brazier was lit there; it was growing chilly outside as the evening darkened. It struck Shakespeare that this was the most generous woman he had ever met; she had even called one of her daughters by the dead queen's name.

Contentment now – and Jean Sutherland was a serene woman – was the apt reward for such generosity of heart. Yet she was not self-important with it; her appearance was that of one to whom nothing has ever happened beyond the usual. He thought of the shrieking Greek mask worn in theatre. Truth hid itself in reality, was not puffed up.

He watched her go to a chest and open it, returning with some matter carefully folded flat in a white linen cloth. Smiling a little, she opened the linen, revealing what lay, like a saint's relic, within. Before his eyes lay the strawberries embroidered by Mary, Queen of Scots.

"Ye ha'e come a fair gait for what the king desires. Oh, we knew. My brother the priest left it wi' me, having got it of Huntly's lady. She left it to his discretion, saying ye had asked concerning it. She didna tak' it upon hersel' to leave it in ither hands."

They spread it out between them. It was stained with sea-water and dried heart's blood; the young earl's. Moray had worn it against him while dying. The priest, all these weeks, had kept it in his pack with the mass-gear.

"It was Patrick our brither who took it frae the earl's body," said Jean. "He is a rough man. He would rifle the body, thinking of gain maybe in silver or coin."

Shakespeare could not take his eyes from the exquisite, ruined handiwork. Up and down England it was known the imprisoned queen had spent many hours consoling herself with embroidery; the same had happened earlier while she was awaiting her son's birth, after the murder of Rizzio. She must have calmed herself with stitching to shut out concern about the coming child; after what had happened with their sword-hilts, would he be deformed?

Strawberries. They would comfort Mary Stuart by reminding her of her own calm, much-loved mother, from whom she had been forced to part, as it turned out for ever, after one brief reunion in France when she was eight. Even then there had been an attempt to poison the royal child who was the sole heir to Scotland. *It cam' wi' a lass, and it will gang wi' a lass*, her dying father James V had said; the first lass had been Marjory Bruce, whose tomb Will had visited at Paisley. Queen Mary herself must have known of that saying, and have wondered if she would die at the birth, if the child within her would be born dead also.

Strawberries; stitched in the scarlet threads, themselves like blood. Mary of Guise had brought new strawberry plants with her to her Scots marriage. They had flourished in the soil of Fife. Thinking of it, Shakespeare remembered hearing of the history of the new, faintly pineapple-flavoured fruit brought from the Americas for the gourmet emperor Charles V. When the French king and his sons were in turn his hostages in Spain, he would treat them as guests, let them sample such fruit. They might well have begged a cutting or two on return, and the cuttings had taken root in French soil, then in Scotland. Strawberries. Small, variously red fruits, tendrils and fanlike leaves; white flowers with a yellow centre; looking up at him through stains of water and blood, the wounds of Christ. How, could he take this to King James as it was now, dark with the heart's blood of a young man he had envied enough to have killed? The queen was to bear a child in early spring. Maybe it would prove a prince. There would be accord between them. This could not be shown; and yet, who else had the right to it?

"I didna try to cleanse it," said Jean Sutherland.

"What am I to do?" he asked. "Am I to tell the king it's found?"

"It is better to let him think it was lost in the fire at Donibristle. There is no need to say which fire."

"Then it must burn?"

"It must burn if ye are to tell the truth. I would not endanger your soul with a lie. The priest my brother thocht the same, but he has aye brought such troubles to me, having much else on his mind. It is a hard thing to destroy it, but we know it has been made, and can remember, though we could never fashion the like again."

Unum solum quid leonem. That, at any rate, was still to be seen in a great house in the south. Mary Stuart had pictured her unknown son as a lion; he had roundabout ways of keeping his kingdom and himself. Yet there was pathos in the man, from affection long denied. He must be permitted to keep what he might from his marriage.

"He loved Esmé greatly," he heard Jean say, as if she read his thoughts. "Huntly's wife, who is Esmé's dochter, told me her father abjured the faith for James's sake, and subscribed to the Kirk. They say it was pretence, but it was not; on his deathbed he refused the sacraments, and directed that his heart should be embalmed and sent to the king."

"Then James has known love." Maybe the casket containing the heart was in the secret cupboard with the poems, in the king's closet at Holyrood. *He was the queen's luve*. No good would come of reminding James forever of the dead Moray.

"Her mother's coffin was all she saw again, returned before she left France to come hame, a widow of eighteen." Jean smoothed the strawberries.

"You loved Mary Stuart," Will said.

"There was no one could fail to love her; even Darnley did sae, but he was young and led away by the Douglases; also, he had the strange illness from his mother, and the king has it forbye, for baith his parents had it; the queen had fainting-fits and a pain in her left side, and headaches often." Moncrieff the physician at Methven had hinted at the same thing. "Bothwell was loyal," said Jean. She always came back to mention of Bothwell; maybe she herself had loved the man, despite his scars or maybe because of them.

She let Will touch the handkerchief. Its silk was stiff with sea-salt and the bloodstains. It still had beauty.

Dy'd in mummy which the skilful conserved Of maidens' hearts. Would the muse never leave him in peace? There was so much crowding in his mind; the old man on the moor, the three witches of Cawdor, the madwoman washing her hands at Glamis, the death of an old king, of gracious Duncan, of the persecuted Church. The image would stay with him, would grow and multiply. He watched without emotion as Jean opened the door of the brazier and stirred its coals with a rod till they burned blue. She handed him the handkerchief, then turned away.

"I will leave ye to do with it as ye will," she said. "I will ken naught. It is time for me to go to my lord, who will be calling for me. He does not like to be lang alane; it brings his sorrows to mind."

"Do any of us lack sorrow?" asked Will. It came to him that his own was long laid aside; once home again, it might return.

"Maybe not," she said, and went out and downstairs, the plain stuff of her skirts making no sound. Will laid the handkerchief against his cheek for instants, then thrust it into the brazier. The dry silk shrivelled and darkened at once, becoming, soon, charred threads without identity. He took the rod and pounded them to nothing. He was the murderer of a fine thing, like the earl of Huntly and his kin. Blood, salt and silk, the many-houred work of a dead queen gone, destroyed in fewer instants than her death; the executioner had had to raise his axe three times. He heard the sick earl's voice sounding, petulantly, from downstairs.

"Jean! Jean! Come to me; I'm solitary. I am not well. I doubt I'll live to see the spring."

Will stared down at the fading ashes. At least he would be able to tell the truth to the king. The strawberry handkerchief had been burnt in the fire. That would leave it to be understood that Moray had not kept it about his person. Later, much later, when the king rode down to London, he would present a play not yet written; a brave, credulous, flawed husband, a wife who was innocent; the gift of a handkerchief spotted with strawberries. He would make it so that the king, if he remembered, would take the whole thing as a compliment. It would take a great deal of work, when he, William Shakespeare, had time.

* * * *

The next he heard of Countess Jean her earl had died, and shortly she was married again, to an old friend, Ogilvy. So much for the clan feud, he thought. The couple stayed on at Dunrobin. It was unlikely that the bothan folk would have wanted to lose their lady's beneficent presence, there in the castle.

Shakespeare had followed the priest's methods and had gone by sea, himself disembarking at Leith while sending the players on as far as Ravenspur, from which place they would find their way home without difficulty. W.H.'s letter received at Elgin had made him anxious to return at once, but it would be discourteous, and a bad presage for the future, not to call on the king at Holyrood with such news as he had.

He avoided Huntly House on this occasion, making use of his old friend the landlady in the Cowgate. There, having rested and eaten, he rehearsed the words with which he would break the news to James Stuart about the burned handkerchief. However once upstairs and sifting through his private gear for laundry, the woman knocked on the door, handing him a wafer that had come. It was sealed with the device of the galley of Lorne.

Shakespeare opened it, half hoping that it was a summons to read to the earl of Argyll. He had avoided the houses of the west coast, where the common folk were mainly Catholic but hauden down, as they said here, by the Kirk. Argyll himself was one of the commissioners. He had evidently heard of the plays, and requested Master Shakespeare to attend him at his town house as soon as might be.

Despite the prospect of profit, Will knew an unwillingness to go. Argyll was loathed in the north parts already for his cruelty to the Clan Gregor, whose grudge was that their lands of Glenorchy had been taken away by those who could produce papers, leaving them homeless.

Argyll himself was still a young man, and was the stepson of the late Regent Moray, whose mantle seemed to have fallen on him. The regent's widow Agnes had married Argyll's father shortly after her husband's murder in 1571. Will reflected idly that that had been the year the pope excommunicated his own queen in England.

He made his way to the Argyll house; it was best to placate great folk. Naturally he would not refuse, though it would delay his departure, a command to read from his plays or verse. He could simulate the voices of the players well enough. However on entering, he was shown into a small room where the earl sat alone, with papers unrolled before him, at a table. He did not look up for moments, as if to remind a strolling player of his place.

Will used the time to reflect on the recurrence of clan features. It had been impossible to mistake a Gordon, and now it was equally impossible to mistake a Campbell. The foxy face, the narrow crafty look, were enhanced by an evident resemblance to the earl's near kinsman Mailleach, the High of Brow. Shakespeare had seen Campbells already at Cawdor. Here was another. The thin arched eyebrows raised themselves slightly in acknowledgment of his presence. The earl of Argyll did not rise.

"I am told you have been in the north of Scotland."

There would have been word from Cawdor. Argyll had not addressed him by name and so he himself used no title. "That is so," he said, and waited. Father James by now would be safe in France. Unwilling to risk being thought secretive, Will added that they had been made most welcome in the north.

"Possibly, as you were in certain company."

"My company always makes watchers merry."

"I refer, as well you know, to that of the Jesuit, James Gordon."

Will remained silent.

"I may inform you," Argyll continued coldly, "that the king has granted me a commission of fire and sword against such persons. It is similar to that granted to the late earl of Moray. Not only has James Gordon of Huntly caused great trouble over the years, reviving papacy in defiance of the late godly religion: there has lately come a rumour of yet another plot with the help of Spain. I would say little of it except that the last was known to all; an attempt was made against England some years back, after the late Queen Mary's death, called the Invincible Armada." Argyll smirked. "Fire and storm, and no doubt the will of providence, gave England then the victory, with the queen's brave speech at Tilbury spurring her sailors on."

"They were commanded by a papist, Lord Howard of Effingham." Will could not resist the comment, knowing he should have held his tongue.

"Do not impede me," said Argyll. "Many Spaniards are known to have been wrecked thereafter on the north coasts, and among the further islands. They will no doubt have spread their beliefs subtly, and obtained help where they might."

Will did not speak again, but remembered Gomez the steward, serving good venison in his bright-patterned tunic. Jean Sutherland had told him, regarding that coloured knitting the island folk had learnt, that one of the patterns was called Crown of Glory, another the Cross. It was a far cry from this chilly probing.

"I must ask for truth in your replies, Shakespeare," continued the earl. "The king is determined to root out this new plot from Spain, which as I say has been rumoured. King Philip's memory is long, and his third queen was a close friend of Mary Stuart in her youth in France. In any case he regards himself as the rightful ruler of England by his former marriage to the late Mary Tudor."

Will replied that he was in the habit of truthfulness, but could give the earl no help in a matter of which he had heard nothing. Father James's silences could however have contained much. He recalled the priest as Grumio, playing bearded in front of the king and court, unrecognised. There might have been a *volte-face* of the kind in which James VI indulged, with regard to his hoped-for English inheritance. One had to play without looking at the cards.

He said now, "I came here to Scotland with my company, and one man falling sick I was joined by another, who said he could learn parts quickly. He played at short notice, I was glad of him, and it was not my concern to ask whence he came. He suited well enough until the sick player grew better. He left us then to go I know not where." All this was the truth, after all. Argyll lifted his high fair brows still further, one higher than the other.

"Ye were seen riding alane in the man's company to Glamis."

"I had a wish to see Glamis. I collect old tales. They told me a king died there at a great age, and I desired to see the place itself." He tried to sound nonchalant, but felt the sweat breaking out on his palms, and hoped it did not show on his forehead. This man would have no mercy. He seemed uncertain, however.

"Then that was all? Ye received no instructions at any time to take back into England? We are aware of your father John Shakespeare's recusant history, and that your mother, Mary Arden, had Somerville kin who were involved in one of the early plots to kill the queen of England. Such information is sent by custom to the commissioners here. Ye ha'e been a marked man since crossing the Border."

"You may examine all my papers, such as they are." What jotting might they not provide that had seemed harmless and private enough? *O blood, blood, blood! She may be honest yet. Have you not seen a handkerchief* . . . Other things of the kind. The only instructions from Father Gordon had been to include secret messages in his plays, but those were yet to be written. He had no certainty, but he did not think he had written down anything incriminating, unless they chose to find it. In future, remembering this fox-faced probing lord, whatever he wrote of the kind would be doubly cryptic.

To his relief, Argyll shrugged. "There is no being upsides wi' a Jesuit; they are replete with guile. Next time Father Gordon of Huntly shows his face on these shores it will mean prison for him. The king cannot be persuaded to harsher measures towards such folk as yet. We will see." The expression on the narrow face grew smug. "They tell me widows in Italy leave these charlatans large sums not only frae the usufructs o' their tochers, but frae the capital itsel', their husbands being deceased. Thankfully the law here is different. Will ye carry letters from mysel' to Lord Burleigh, at his house in the Strand?"

Will knew this was a deliberate attempt to implicate him. He prevaricated by saying that he had not perhaps intended going straight to London; he must visit Stratford and his family. "I have not seen my son since he was newborn," he said, and made himself smile. "Such is the life of a player."

"Ye chose the life, however, as opposed to schoolmastering, I believe."

To Will's surprise, he then asked if a play could be read here at his house before Shakespeare departed. "My young sister Annas needs diversion; she is motherless, and we have a young guest who is likewise, one ye will ha'e seen at the queen's court being daughter to the late earl of Moray." His lips compressed themselves, obviously remembering the murder and Huntly's part in it. "The queen has a care to several such young folk, but is returned to Stirling to await her lying-in, as ye will ken." It was evident that he credited Will with his own omniscience. To a certain extent he was justified; keeping one's ear to the ground produced, in the end, the same result, for less money, than paying a network of informers.

In Argyll's house that evening, Will read aloud a tentative play he had not yet produced. It concerned the confusion of identities of twins. He was not sure how a worldly audience would receive it, but these were young, the earl himself not having deigned to appear. In any case Argyll would doubtfully pay much; no doubt he had inherited his mother's acquisitiveness as well as the mantle of godly sobriety of her first spouse, the long-dead Regent Moray. Agnes Keith herself was dead; those who watched were of the next generation.

They were handsomely dressed, and must be known to the king and queen. A particularly fine pair Will noticed at once, seated side by side; and knew them for Ruthvens. The girl had been with the queen that time at Dunfermline, and the boy had been the younger of the two Gowrie brothers met at Holyrood. He tried to recall their mother Dorothea, but could remember only sadness. No doubt she still lived on, in the houses of kin.

He was suddenly assailed by a feeling of intense danger. In the midst of the struggles and laughter at the tying up of Antipholus, he was almost convinced that a dagger was at his back; but there was no one behind him. He became aware that the danger was not to himself. Before his eyes was the coat of arms with the coronet, and *Deid Schaw*. A voice was calling out "Help! Help! Murder," in a smothered fashion as though a hand was laid across its mouth. It seemed to come from an upper window, and he recognised the voice as the king's.

It must have been a waking dream, of a kind to which he was not prone. It occurred to him that he had had little sleep on the journey, and had not taken time to rest today. The sound of his own voice had continued, the errors were duly disentangled to more laughter; why did he think of two young bodies already dead? He shook himself free of the sensation, and of the smell of death not recent, as if, like the Bonnie Earl, they had been conveyed from one place to another, then exposed. He found himself back among the present audience, the sound of applause, his own final bow. A young girl with a vacant face smiled on. He knew from her features that this was Annas Campbell. The dead young earl of Moray's daughter Margaret, whom he remembered, came to him then, taking Agnes Keith's daughter by the limp hand; the girl had not all her wits.

"Annas and I like to dress up," said Margaret Stewart. Will not ye come and see our box, Maister Shakespeare? There are many things in it that would gladden your folk for the plays, but they're not mine to give."

He was led upstairs, not unwillingly; he was still shaken in his own mind and for once, did not want solitude. What must happen must happen, as with the Greeks. The tragedy centred on the Gowries, as if the execution of their father had not been enough. The beautiful earl and his brother, and the young girls, and others he had not met – there were twelve still living – would suffer for their name, a name the king had already silenced with regard to the tower where he had been kept prisoner a year. Ruthven tower was now Huntingtower. The owners of the name would die. He felt certain of it, and that the full truth would never be openly known.

He saw the girls open a chest in the upstairs room, which

looked out on the street. The nurse who looked after poor Annas bobbed and went respectfully away. Caps and ruffs of an older time were brought out, having long lost their freshness; they had once been crisp. The present earl of Argyll's mother had been known to help herself copiously to the possessions of the fugitive queen of Scots, her then husband Moray having safely won Langside.

Without question some of these things could have belonged only to a queen; lace of such delicacy could only have come from France. The wired, winged caps resembled those in portraits of Mary Stuart he had seen in certain houses, one belonging to the executed duke of Norfolk, Arundel's father. Such caps had once enclosed, heart-shaped, that red-gold head whose long lock of severed hair Lord Paisley carried still. The ruffs had encircled the slender neck also severed, less quickly, by the axe at Fotheringay.

Of jewellery there was of course none. It would be locked up securely in Argyll's coffers or, just possibly, in those of his late half-sister at Doune. The daughter of Moray was with them now. He wondered what the future held for her, with her notable beauty. He hoped it held happiness.

He resisted the temptation to filch something, anything, to take to the king in memory of his mother. After all the property was stolen already. However the young folk might be blamed, so Will kept his fingers from the wired lace. As it turned out, Margaret Stewart brought young Annas presently, ludicrously attired in one of the caps. She was holding something in her hand. The noise of the street lessened as a horse and cart passed by below, laden with turnips, the owner shouting his wares.

"Turnerups! Turnerups!" A wicked pun occurred to Will, in the way such things came to him unbidden. Moray's lovely and kind-hearted young daughter was saying something. He felt ashamed of himself.

"Annas would like ye to ha'e this in a gift to take back to England, would ye no', Annas? She liked the play." Annas smiled on, evidently unable to speak. "It was the dead queen's," said Margaret, "and hath no fellow, for we ha'e sought often."

Annas held out a small high-heeled shoe, in colour a faded green. The lining had once been rose-colour, by now in shreds. There was gold embroidery, tarnished somewhat, on the front, showing twined initials, M and FII, and a lily and crown.

"That was for the late queen and the young king o' France, her first husband," Margaret said. The foot the shoe had fitted must have been incredibly small. Shakespeare took the gift reverently, and kissed poor Annas Campbell's hands as though she were indeed the queen whose cap she wore.

Turning away with it stowed in his doublet, Will saw Beatrix Ruthven leaning against the door, watching. It seemed a fact here that one was always watched, but she had heard the giving of the queen's shoe. She was smiling, and he could picture her mother Dorothea doing so in old days, when she was happy with her earl and their family. "Write mair plays, Maister Shakespeare," Beatrix said. "One day we may come to see them in London."

It was an unguarded speech, of the kind Dorothea Gowrie must herself often have made. Will knew this daughter of hers would never see London. Whatever her fate was to be, it was adverse, in her stars; at worst, to be put out on the streets without sustenance, at best to make a marriage far beneath her. He could do nothing to prevent any of it. He made his farewells and left. He had yet to see the king.

*   *   *   *

Shakespeare met King James VI for the last time before they were to meet again in London, the king by then as James VI and I, the playwright a well-known and respected figure with a house in Stratford which only daughters would inherit; his son Hamnet had died at six years old. The king's heir, a prince born strong and healthy at Stirling in February, was to die also, before his father.

Nobody was to know that yet. Will was shown to the familiar closet, where the royal eyes surveyed him, slightly blurred. James had been taught to drink deep in Denmark on his wedding journey, and the habit had grown with the years. He spoke of the handkerchief at once.

"Ye made diligent search, mon? Ye were in mony houses in the north. There is trouble brewing there wi' Crawford turned papist. He and Huntly and Erroll may combine to our undoing. I may ride there mysel' once my Annie is delivered o' our bairn. Had ye word o' the handkerchief?"

Shakespeare said nothing, but handed over a small green shoe. Tears rose in the king's eyes, which were not strictly aligned. He turned to his cupboard, where he kept his secret matters, and brought out a casket of wrought silver and gold.

"Place it here. This is the heart o' Esmé Stuart, wha would ha'e got my royal mither out o' her prison to rule alongside mysel'. That was his dream, but it cam' tae nocht wi' his deith. It is fitting that Mary Stuart's shoe should stay close to't."

Will placed the shoe beside the reliquary. It was unlikely that Mary and her son would have ruled together peaceably, but the stuff of dreams should not be torn. He recalled seeing, at Strathbogie, a double portrait of the queen and her son, who had never met again in life; James had been wearing the oriflamme of France on his head, an unlikely possibility. He had resembled, at the age of about seventeen, his father Darnley.

"The handkerchief burned," said Will. It was best to state it. James Stuart was gazing down at the shoe and the heart. He did not look up.

"Ye ha'e done weel," he said. "There is siller for ye at the outgait."

Shakespeare bowed, turned and went.

On his way home, having steered the troupe safely through the debatable lands, he paused at Peterborough once again. This time he did no more than glance at the long coffin of Mary, Queen of Scots. He went to another nearby, that of Catharine of Aragon, Henry VIII's stubborn Spanish wife, beloved in her time in England, by now almost forgotten. Will had not forgotten her, or her story; it had often occurred to him that he might write a play about the present queen's father. At that rate he must vaunt Anne Boleyn, the queen's mother; yet at the same time he was thinking of her as the wicked Lady Macbeth. That was his trade, no doubt, to put folk into a melting-pot, distort the truth to divert an audience. This woman, lying dead here for nigh on sixty years, had never distorted truth.

He laid his hand on the tomb, as if to bring himself to her soul's understanding. He would give her a fine speech at the trial; that was recorded of her. Otherwise the play must flatter his queen. "I am sorry," he said aloud, hearing his voice echo, Lady Macbeth would perhaps atone. No doubt Macbeth and his wife had been wholesome enough; he would turn them into totally different people. Pilate had asked what truth was. Pilate would have saved Christ. Had he done so, mankind would not have been saved. Everything had been intended from the beginning of the world; and yet, man had his freedom.

He found himself wondering why Catharine had lost so many children by her king. At the same time, Margaret Tudor was bearing dead children to James IV. That king, as he had learnt in Scotland, had nevertheless had healthy bastards. The sickness must have been in the Tudor blood. It had descended to James V, to his daughter, to her bridegroom Darnley through his mother; to the enigma who was James VI. Before that, long before, Catharine had earned her king's resentment for being a better general than he was; she had won Flodden for England, proud of being like her mother, the warlike Isabella of Castile; but Henry VIII, then in France, had won no such victory. They'd said that was when the differences began between the pair; that, and a lack of heirs. It was to be hoped Queen Anna's children would live. Perhaps the Danish blood would bring new strength.

Catharine, who had loved her king, had promised to send him a piece of the king of Scots' bloodstained coat after Flodden. There was a mystery there he'd learned of in the north. James IV had had a quarrel with the earl of Home, who had taunted him, saying it was safe enough to fight in royal cognizance. The king had sworn to fight without it, in other words clad like any knight. Whatever Catharine had sent to Henry VIII at Térouenne had not, after all, been a piece of the royal coat, with the lions of Scotland. It might have been a strip cut from the bloodstained shirt. James had fought valiantly, falling at last a lance's length from old Surrey the English commander. Henry VIII had refused his body Christian burial. The more one thought of the queen's father the less one liked him; but at some time, he must write that play also. It would help to feed his family. Soon now, he would see them again.

The more he thought of it, the more *Macbeth* became the secret version of the play about the queen's father. Only the other could be played in her lifetime. Henry VIII, at first a devoted son of the pope, given the title (which he had kept) of Defender of the Faith for his war against France and the victory of Flodden, sent the great accolade of the Golden Rose, had allowed his passion for a woman, his wish for an heir, to warp his nature. From tentative beginnings he had committed increasing crimes, murders, thefts for greed. He had destroyed, to the best of his ability, any power the old faith possessed in England while still considering himself beyond censure. He had become arrogant, callous and cruel. He had ended by killing the woman who had led him on, while she herself had grown half-mad with remorse at the last.

Yes, it would do. He could portray Henry VIII as the murderer he was, his lady as a fiend who changed to a crazed sleepwalker, washing her hands to rid them of blood. *Who would have thought the old man had so much blood in him?* The Church, gracious Duncan; the old, old king. One could play with the facts of history to portray a truth. Catharine of Aragon need no longer reproach him from her forgotten tomb in Peterborough.

He wondered if, when James VI rode south as king of England, he would honour his mother's remains in any way. One could never be certain.

Will heard several things on return to England by Christmas. Queen Anna gave birth to Prince Henry Frederick safely in February. Thereafter, her lord and king excelled himself by riding up to Aberdeen with armed support against the rebel lords Huntly, Erroll and Crawford, who had broken out in rebellion over the state of affairs regarding their religion. They won a skirmish at Glenlivet, but it grew with much telling into a battle the king had won for himself.

He took his revenge by burning the fine new house of Strathbogie, thereby humbling the Cock o' the North and silencing tongues which said he would never raise a hand against Huntly. Nonetheless James would never be able entirely to subdue his affection for that unlikely object of it. Huntly fled abroad, then returned without asking, made pretence to adopt the king's new version of the reformed faith, but died a papist with full rites at Elgin in the fulness of time.

By then, there had long been an annual thanksgiving in Scotland for the king's deliverance from the Gowries. He had gone to dine at Perth with the returned young earl, lately the town's provost, and his brother. After dinner they had gone upstairs. Shortly the king's face was seen at an upper window, shouting for help against murder. When they reached him from the street, it was to find the earl and his brother dead of stab wounds, while the king babbled of a giant knight in black armour nobody else, then or later, saw.

The two young bodies were conveyed to Edinburgh, hanged and quartered – there was no disembowelling in Scotland – and exposed as those of traitors, more safely in the capital as the good citizens of Perth were angry at the death of their popular young provost. Hearing of all of it, Shakespeare put together what he knew. James Stuart, on entering to dine, must have seen the gleaming coronet; but that would merely inflame an anger already there. It was said the earl of Gowrie had made overtures of marriage to the strictly watched Lady Arbell Stuart, daughter of Darnley's dead brother and an heir to the English throne. Taken together, and with the king's later treatment of Arbell, the two pointers might suffice. James VI wanted the Crown of England at all costs, riding down three years afterwards at leisure on hunting-trips arranged by his eager English hosts, steeping his weak legs – he was a centaur in the saddle, however – at each day's end in the warm blood of slaughtered deer. He had obtained his heart's desire; he was king of the united kingdoms, so long at odds with one another, and he had won them not by war, but by keeping his tongue inside his mouth. It was maybe not the way of his ancestors, but his ancestors were dead; dead like the Gowries. To have made overtures to the Lady Arbell! He would keep her under his eye, in attendance on the queen. One must still keep watch. The tale from Traquair must be forgotten.

However the Gowries were themselves forgotten in the greater deliverance, if it was one, from gunpowder such as had been intended to destroy the king's father at Kirk o' Field. Many said at the time that the supposed Gunpowder Plot of 1605 was a contrivance of Cecil's own, by then the king's beagle, set on foot by a forged letter. Nevertheless each year thereafter the dummy of Guy Fawkes, a young man tortured beyond recognition before death with the rest on the scaffold, burned in popular fires up and down England, and the papists were held to blame.

About then, Will received a letter from W.H., by then third earl, who asked him to burn it as soon as read.

It seemed foolish and irrelevant in face of the late plot, the hanging of Father Garnet, whose messages Will already occupied, inserting them in the by now sketched *Macbeth*, possible to produce by this time with the death of the old queen. He brought in sobriquets, symbols, a drunken porter whose ramblings could be denied as meaning anything if trouble arose, while conveying much to those who understood. He glanced at W.H.'s letter, then put it aside. What it concerned itself with no longer mattered. However it brought back the Scottish journey, and the dead Gowries, even the dead earl of Moray. The younger Ruthven brothers had fled to England, one of them from school; but the king had had them imprisoned as soon as he arrived. The sisters had been dismissed from court, and had no home. He learned later on that Queen Anna helped them secretly with money. The king's strange memory retained small things. It would perhaps be better if he could allow himself to blot them out. Nobody now could assail his position; and yet, his treatment of the Lady Arbell echoed that of the Ruthvens. Nothing would be forgotten by James VI and I; not even what lay at the back of his own mind and none other's. Too much of his time was spent idly; he admitted it himself; but said that when he worked at all, he became extremely diligent.

Shakespeare turned away from the thought of the king, and took up W.H.'s letter again. *The rumour goes that the Gowrie matter was set on foot by reason of the queen's passing by in the palace garden in Scotland before they came south, and having with her one of the young Ruthven women, who led her to her brother asleep under a tree. The queen exclaimed at his beauty, and tied a silver ribbon the king had given her about his neck. That is said to be the reason for rooting out the whole clan and forbidding the name, as has happened also to the Clan Gregor up there; their leader was executed in Edinburgh, and the bodies of the two young Ruthvens used as you know. There are other reasons stated for the king's action, one of which I will tell you when we meet; but I do not myself believe that a mother of three, which the queen was even by then, would stoop to such a frolic with so young a man, though one never knows the follies of women. The last Ruthven brother is in the Tower, and looks not to come out.* He ended with friendly messages. Will burned the letter. The tale about the silver ribbon was no more than an echo of the earlier one about the strawberry handkerchief, and had perhaps been put about by the king himself.

Will went out to walk in his Stratford garden, bending to sniff the sweet scent of the lavender bushes he had himself planted; they drove away the remembered smell of blood. *O blood, blood, blood! Othello* itself had been as successful as *Macbeth*: he had performed both before James in person, with no complaints evident about the mention of a strawberry handkerchief. There must be many matters since then in the king's mind. He and the queen had made a triumphal entry together beneath a great arch designed for them in London. The queen had interested herself greatly in masques. He himself was growing too set in his ways to take to this new medium. He had heard one more piece of gossip about Danish Anna it was best not to repeat; evidently she had had a secret friendship at the time, with Francis Bothwell; it might not have been accident that her door was bolted at the time of his assailing of the king, kneeling with sword drawn. By now, Bothwell was dead miserably in Naples, having fled to France, been advised to leave there for Spain after a duel, and finally earned a living of sorts by teaching sword-play and telling fortunes. It was a sorry end for one who had had a fair beginning. The Kirk's commissioners had had to take pity on one of his daughters, who was left near starvation.

Queens were blamed for much. Anna of Denmark was not the fool men thought her. She had given quiet advice to the king over the years, which at times he took. She had long since saved Willie Logie, by means of his sweetheart Margaret Twinelace, by enabling the young man to tiptoe out from prison through the very room where she and the king shared a bed. That had been at the time of the Gowrie affair, but James had forgiven in that instance, and the pair were married.

He was married, after all, himself. He had settled down

again with his wife. They said the queen was ill, and would soon die. They said also that she had considered becoming a papist. He himself would not live long, and had done what he might by messages in his plays, but three years ago, in Scotland, the king had hanged young Father John Ogilvie, after enjoying his company secretly two months in Whitehall.

Everywhere was shifting sand. They had married the Bonnie Earl's lovely young daughter to old Lord Howard of Effingham, victor long ago against the Armada. The marriage of January and May seemed to be content enough; she made him a faithful wife. There was no story there even Chaucer could devise, though they had unwittingly offended the old lord with finger-language when the queen's brother, speaking no English, came over from Denmark and everybody got drunk.

He himself had made a play over another marriage, at the time Prince Henry Frederick died and his sister Elizabeth, who in charm and features resembled the king's mother Mary Queen of Scots – that put paid to stories of a dead baby in a wall – became the wife of the young Count Palatine. He had written a play called *The Tempest* and had put King James openly in it as a wise scholar, learned in magic, with the Princess Elizabeth as Miranda and the young Palatine as Ferdinand. The king had been pleased with the play, and maybe the queen, who had been against the marriage as not high enough in birth for her daughter, was partly consoled.

These were great matters. Otherwise it was time he, William Shakespeare, was dead. He would die a papist; and hoped none would disturb his bones. There had been a comet lately blazing in the night sky, whether for his own dying or the queen's he did not know. The king, in the midst of one of the attacks of strange illness he had from both parents, and which would prevent his attending Anna's funeral, had written certain lines ready for it. Will had heard the first of them. *Thee the great God invited by a star.* The king had been fond, after all, of his Annie, with her tiny ridiculous hats and huge farthingales, and her debts and her snobberies. The prince's death had drawn them together at the end. The king's young men took the place of sons to him rather than lovers. Of all his family, there was only one son left, Prince Charles. He had overcome his stammer and could master a stallion. It would be a different reign, and he, Will, did not want to see it, though it was possible there might be mercy shown at last to the Ruthvens. One was still in the Tower. Lady Arbell had died there three years ago, they said insane; small wonder if so, she had paid for being born niece to Darnley, and had finally made an imprudent love-match. The king had caught her escaping overseas, and had imprisoned her. Will recalled her pale face and bright hair, riding earlier behind the queen on some court progress. Like them all she had the old illness, handed down from Queen Margaret Tudor. That Thistle and Rose marriage had shed much blood, caused much grief, but now, at last, the lands were under one king.

Well, he, William Shakespeare, had learned much and must keep silent about a good deal. He would die in the same year as the queen. The secret messages Father Huntly had suggested are in his plays for those who care to understand them. Those who do not will find much else to divert them.